INDIA AND THE PRE-REQUISITES OF COMMUNISM

MAVEN BOOKS

INDIA AND THE PRE-REQUISITES OF COMMUNISM

Dr. B. R. AMBEDKAR

MAVEN BOOKS

Chennai   New Delhi

MAVEN BOOKS

An Imprint of MJP Publishers

ISBN 9789388191784 **Maven Books**

All rights reserved   No. 44, Nallathambi Street,
Printed and bound in India   Triplicane, Chennai 600 005

MJP 668   © Publishers, 2024

Publisher : C. Janarthanan

PUBLISHER'S NOTE

The legacy of a country is in its varied cultural heritage, historical literature, developments in the field of economy and science. The top nations in the world are competing in the field of science, economy and literature. This vast legacy has to be conserved and documented so that it can be bestowed to the future generation. The knowledge of this legacy is slowly getting perished in the present generation due to lack of documentation.

Keeping this in mind, the concern with retrospective acquiring of rare books has been accented recently by the burgeoning reprint industry. Maven Books is gratified to retrieve the rare collections with a view to bring back those books that were landmarks in their time.

In this effort, a series of rare books would be republished under the banner, "Maven Books". The books in the reprint series have been carefully selected for their contemporary usefulness as well as their historical importance within the intellectual. We reconstruct the book with slight enhancements made for better presentation, without affecting the contents of the original edition.

Most of the works selected for republishing covers a huge range of subjects, from history to anthropology. We believe this reprint edition will be a service to the numerous researchers and practitioners active in this fascinating field. We allow readers to experience the wonder of peering into a scholarly work of the highest order and seminal significance.

Maven Books

EDITOR'S NOTE

Editorial Note for the manuscript published in the Dr. Babasaheb Ambedkar: Writings and Speeches, Vol. 3 by the Government of Maharashtra:

We are reproducing here the text of Chapter One and Two of ' The Hindu Social Order '. This Chapter seems to be a part of the book entitled ' India and Communism '. From the contents on the first page of the typed script, we find that Dr. Ambedkar had divided the whole book " India and Communism " into three parts. The first part was captioned as ' The Prerequisites of Communism '. This part was to have three Chapters but we could not find any of these Chapters in Dr. Ambedkar's papers. So far as the part Two is concerned which is titled " India and the Pre-requisites of Communism ", only Chapter Four entitled, " Hindu Social Order "has been found in a well bound register. This Chapter has two sub-titles as follows: —

I—Hindu Social Order: Its Essential Principles, and II— The Hindu Social Order: Its Unique Features. No other chapters on the subjects mentioned in the table of contents of this book were found.

CONTENTS

CHAPTER 1

The Hindu Social Order: It's Essential Principles

I

What is the character of the Hindu Social Order? Is it a free social order? To answer this question, some idea of what constitutes a free social order is necessary. Fortunately, the matter is not one of controversy. Since the days of the French Revolution there is no difference as to the essentials of a free social order. There may be more but two are fundamental. Generally speaking, they are two. The first is that the individual is an end in him self and that the aim and object of society is the growth of the individual and the development of his personality. Society is not above the individual and if the individual has to subordinate himself to society, it is because such subordination is for his betterment and only to the extent necessary.

The second essential is that the terms of associated life between members of society must be regarded by consideration founded on liberty, equality and fraternity.

Why are these two essentials fundamental to a free social order? Why must the individual be the end and not the means of all social purposes? For an answer to this question, it is necessary to realise what we precisely mean when we speak of the human person. Why should we sacrifice our most precious possessions and our lives to defend the rights of the human person? No better answer to this question can be found than what is given by Prof. Jacques Maritain. As Prof. Maritain in his essay on ' The Conquest of Freedom '[1] says:-

" What do we mean precisely when we speak of the human person? When we say that a man is a person, we do not mean merely that he is an individual, in the sense that an atom, a blade of grass, a fly, or an elephant is an individual. Man is an individual who holds himself in hand by his intelligence and his will; he exists not merely in a physical fashion. He has spiritual super-existence through knowledge and love, so that he is, in a way, a universe in himself, a microcosms, in which the great universe in its entirety can be encompassed through knowledge.

By love he can give himself completely to beings who are to him, as it were, other selves. For this relation no equivalent can be found in the physical world. The human person possesses these characteristics because in the last analysis man, this flesh and these perishable bones which are animated and activated by a divine fire, exists 'from the womb to the grave ' by virtue of the existence itself of his soul, which dominates time and death. Spirit is the root of personality. The notion of personality thus involves that of totality and independence, no matter how poor and crushed a person may be, he is a whole, and as a person subsistent in an independent manner. To say that a man is a person is to say that in the depth of his being he is more a whole than a part and more independent than servile. It is to say that he is a minute fragment of matter that is at the same time a universe, a beggar who participates in the absolute being, mortal flesh whose value is external and a bit of straw into which heaven enters. It is this metaphysical mystery that religious thought designates when it says that the person is the image of God. The value of the person, his dignity and rights, belong to the order of things naturally sacred which bear the imprint of the Father of Being, and which have in him the end of their movement. " Why

---

1   Freedom—It's meaning by Ruth Nanda Kishen. p. 214.

is Equality essential? The best exposition of the subject is by Prof. Beard in his essay on ' Freedom in Political Thought ' and I shall do no more than quote him. Says Prof. Beard[2]: —

"The term 'Equality' is unfortunate, but no other word can be found as a substitute. Equality means ' exactly the same or equivalent in measure, amount, number, degree, value, or quality ". It is a term exact enough in physics and mathematics, but obviously inexact when applied to human beings. What is meant by writers who have gone deepest into the subject is that human beings possess, in degree and kind, fundamental characteristics that are common to humanity. These writers hold that when humanity is stripped of extrinsic goods and conventions incidental to time and place, it reveals essential characteristics so widely distributed as to partake of universality. Whether these characteristics be called primordial qualities, biological necessities, residues or any other name matters little. No one can truthfully deny that they do exist. It is easy to point out inequalities in physical strength, in artistic skill, in material wealth, or in mental capacity, but this too is a matter of emphasis. At the end it remains a fact that fundamental Characteristics appear in all human beings. Their nature and manifestations are summed up in the phrase ' moral equality '.

Emphasis must be placed on the term ' moral '. From time immemorial it has been the fashion of critics to point out the obvious facts that in physical strength, talents, and wealth, human beings are not equal. The criticism is both gratuitous and irrelevant. No rational exponent of moral equality has even disputed the existence of obvious inequalities among human beings, even when he has pointed out inequalities, which may be ascribed to tyranny or institutional prescriptions. The Declaration of Independence does not assert that all men are equal; it proclaims that they are ' created ' equal.

In essence the phrase ' moral equality ' asserts in ethical value, a belief to be sustained, and recognition of rights to be respected.

---

2   Freedom—Its Meaning—pp. 11-13.

Its validity cannot be demonstrated as a problem in mathematics can be demonstrated. It is asserted against inequalities in physical strength, talents, industry, and wealth. It denied that superior physical strength has a moral right to kill, eat, or oppress human beings merely because it is superior. To talents and wealth, the ideal of moral equality makes a similar denial of right. And indeed few can imagine themselves to have superior physical strength, talents and wealth will withhold from inferiors all moral rights. In such circumstances government and wealth would go to superior physical strength; while virtue and talents would serve the brute man, as accomplished Greek slaves served the whims, passions and desires to Roman conquerors. When the last bitter word of criticism has been uttered against the ideal of moral equality, there remains something in it which all, except things, must accept and in practice do accept, despite their sheers and protests. A society without any respect for human personalities is a band of robbers. "

Why is Fraternity essential?

Fraternity is the name for the disposition of an individual to treat men as the object of reverence and love and the desire to be in unity with his fellow beings. This statement is well expressed by Paul when he said ' Of one blood are all nations of men. There is neither Jew nor Greek, neither bond nor free, neither male nor female; for yet are ail one in Christ Jesus. ' Equally well was it expressed when the Pilgrim Fathers on their landing at Plymouth said: " We are knit together as a body in the most sacred covenant of the Lord. . . . by virtue of which we hold ourselves tied to all care of each others' good and of the whole. " These sentiments are of the essence of fraternity. Fraternity strengthens socialites and gives to each individual a stronger personal interest in practically consulting the welfare of others. It leads him to identify his feelings more and more with their good, or at least with an even greater degree of practical consideration for it. With a disposition to fraternity he comes as though instructively to be conscious of him as being one who of course pays a regard to others. The good of others becomes to him a thing naturally and necessarily to be attended to like any of the physical conditions of our existence. Where people do not feel that entire sympathy with all others, concordance in the general direction of their conduct is impossible. For a person in whom social feeling is not developed cannot but bring himself to think of the rest of his fellow-beings as rivals struggling with him for the means of happiness when he must endeavour to defeat in order that he may succeed in himself.

What is Liberty and why is it essential in a free social order?

Liberty falls under two classes. There is civil liberty and there is political liberty. Civil liberty refers to (1) liberty of movement which is another name for freedom from arrest without due process of law (2) liberty of speech (which of course includes liberty of thought, liberty of reading, writing and discussion) and (3) liberty of action.

The first kind of liberty is of course fundamental. Not only fundamental it is also most essential. About its value, there can be no manner of doubt. The second kind of liberty, which may be called freedom of opinion, is important for many reasons. It is a necessary condition of all progress intellectual, moral, political and social. Where it does not exist the status quo becomes stereotyped and all originality even the most necessary is discouraged. Liberty of action means doing what one likes to do. It is not enough that liberty of action should be formal. It must be real. So understood liberty of action means effective power to do specific things. There is no freedom where there are no means of taking advantage of it. Real liberty of action exists only where exploitation has been annihilated, where no suppression of one class by another exists, where there is no unemployment, no poverty and where a person is free from the fear of losing his job, his home and his food as a consequence of his action.

Political liberty consists in the right of the individual to share in the framing of laws and in the making and unmaking of governments. Governments are instituted for securing to men certain unalienable rights such as life, liberty and pursuit of happiness. Government must, therefore, derive its powers from those whose rights it is charged with the duty to protect. This is what is meant when it is said that the existence, power and authority of the Government must be derived from the consent of the governed. Political liberty is really a deduction from the principle of human personality and equality. For it implies that all political authority is derived from the people that the people are capable of directing and controlling their public as well as private lives to ends determined by themselves and by none else.

These two tenets of a free social order are integrally connected. They are non-separable. Once the first tenet is admitted, the second tenet automatically follows. Once the sacredness of human personality is admitted the necessity of liberty, equality and fraternity must also be admitted as the proper climate for the development of personality.

II

How far does the Hindu social order recognise these tenets? The inquiry is necessary. For it is only in so far as it recognises these tenets that it will have the title to be called a free social order.

Does the Hindu social order recognise the individual?

Does it recognise his distinctiveness his moral responsibility? Does it recognise him as an end in himself, as a subject not merely of disabilities but also of rights even against the State? As a starting point for the discussion of the subject one may begin by referring to the words of the exodus where Jehova says to Ezekiel:—

"Behold! All souls are mine; as the soul of the Father, so also the soul of the son is mine; the soul that sinister, it shall die. .. .. the son shall not bear the iniquity of the Father, neither shall the father bear the iniquity of the son; the righteousness of the righteous shall be upon him, and the wickedness of the wicked upon him." Here is emphasised the distinctiveness of the individual and his moral responsibility. The Hindu social order does not recognise the individual as a centre of social purpose. For the Hindu social order is based primarily on class or Varna and not on individuals. Originally and formally the Hindu social order recognised four classes: (1) Brahmins, (2) Kshatriyas (3) Vaishyas and (4) Shudras. Today it consists of five classes, the fifth being called the Panchamas or Untouchables. The unit of Hindu society is not the individual Brahmin or the individual Kshatriya or the individual Vaishya or the individual Shudra or the individual Panchama. Even the family is not regarded by the Hindu social order as the unit of society except for the purposes of marriage and inheritance The unit of Hindu society is the class or Varna to use the Hindu technical name for class. In the Hindu social order, there is no room for individual merit and no consideration of individual justice. If the individual has a privilege it is not because it is due to him personally. The privilege goes with the class and if he is found to enjoy it, it is because he belongs to that class. Countrywide, if an individual is suffering from a wrong, it is not because he by his conduct deserves it. The disability is the disability imposed upon the class and if he is found to be labouring under it, it is because he belongs to that class.

Does the Hindu social order recognise fraternity?

The Hindus like the Christians and the Muslims do believe that men are created by God. But while the Christians and the Muslims accept this as the whole truth the Hindus believe that this is only part of the truth. According to them, the whole truth consists of two parts. The first part is that men are created by God. The second part is that God created different men from different parts of his divine body.

The Hindus regard the second part as more important and more fundamental than the first.

The Hindu social order is based on the doctrine that men are created from the different parts of the divinity and therefore the view expressed by Paul or the Pilgrim Fathers has no place in it. The Brahmin is no brother to the Kshatriya because the former is born from the mouth of the divinity while the latter is from the arms. The Kshatriya is no brother to the Vaishya because the former is born from the arms and the latter from his thighs. As no one is a brother to the other, no one is the keeper of the other.

The doctrine that the different classes were created from different parts of the Divine body has generated the belief that it must be divine will that they should remain separate and distinct. It is this belief which has created in the Hindu an instinct to be different, to be separate and to be distinct from the rest of his fellow Hindus. Compare the following rules in the Manu Smriti regarding the Upanayan or the Investiture of a body with the sacred thread :—

II. 36. " In the eighth year after conception, one should perform the initiation (Upanayan) of a Brahmani in the eleventh after conception (that) of a Kshatriya but in the twelfth that of a Vaishya. "

II. 41. "Let students according to the order (of their castes), wear (as upper dressed) the skins of black antelope, spotted deer, and he-goats and (lower garments) made of hemp, flex or wool. "

II. 42. " The girdle of a Brahmana shall consist of a triple cord of Munga grass, smooth and soft (that) of a Kshatriya, of a bowstring, made of Murva fibres (that) of a Vaishya of hempen threads.

II. 43. "If Munga grass (and soforth) be not procurable, (the girdles) may be made of kusa, Asmantaka, and Belbaga (fibres) with a single threefold knot, or with three or five (knots according to the custom of the family. "

II. 44. "The sacrificial string of a Brahmana shall be made of cotton (shall be) twisted to the right, (and consist) of three threads, that of a Kshatriya of hempen threads, and that of a Vaishya of woolen threads.

II. 45. " A Brahamana shall carry according to sacred law a staff of Bilva or Palasa, a Kshatriya of Vata or Khadira; and a Vaishya of Pillu or Udumbara. "

II. 46. " The staff of a Brahmana shall be made of such length as to reach the end of his hair; that of a Kshatriya to reach his forehead ; and that of a Vaishya to reach the tip of his nose. "

II. 48. " Having taken a staff according to his choice having worshipped the Sun and walked round the fire, turning his right hand towards it (the student) should beg alms according to the prescribed rule. "

II. 49. " An initiated Brahmana should beg, beginning his request with the word lady (bhavati); a Kshatriya placing the word lady in the middle, but a Vaishya placing it at the end of the formula. "

On reading this one may well ask the reasons for such distinctions. The above rules refer to students or what are called Bramhacharia ready to enter upon the study of the Vedas. Why should there be these distinctions? Why should the ages of Upanayana of the Brahmin boy differ from that of the Kshatriya or Vaishya? Why should their garments be of different kind? Why should their materials of girdle cords be different? Why should the material of strings be different? Why should their staves be of different trees? Why should their staves differ in length? Why in uttering the formula for asking alms they should place the word ' Bhavathi ' in different places? These differences are not necessary nor advantageous. The only answer is that they are the result of the Hindu instinct to be different from his fellow which has resulted from the belief of people being innately different owing to their being created from different parts of the divine body.

It is also the Hindu instinct due to the same belief never to overlook a difference if it does exist but to emphasise it, recognise it and to blazon it forth. If there is caste its existence must be signalised by a distinguishing headdress and by a distinguishing name. If there is a sect it must have its head mark. There are 92 sects in India. Each has a separate mark of itself. To invent 92 marks each one different from the other is a colossal business. The very impossibility of it would have made the most ingenious person to give up the task. Yet, the Hindus have accomplished it as may be seen from the pictorial representation of these marks given by Moore in his Hindu Pantheon.

The most extensive and wild manifestation of this spirit of isolation and separation is of course the caste-system. It is understandable that caste in a single number cannot exist. Caste can exist only in plural number. There can be castes. But there cannot be such a thing as a caste. But granting that theoretically castes must exist in plural number how many castes should there be ? Originally, there were four only. Today, how many are there? It. is estimated that the total is not less than 2000. It might be 3000. This is not the only staggering aspect of this fact. There are others. Castes are divided into sub-castes. Their number is legion. The total population of the Brahmin castes is about a crore and a half. But there are 1886 sub-castes of Brahmin caste!! In the Punjab alone, the Saraswat Brahmans are divided into 469 sub-castes. The Kayasthas of Punjab are divided into 890 sub-castes!! One could go on giving figures to show this infinite process of splitting social life into small fragments. The splitting process has made a social life quite impossible. It has made the castes split into such small fragments that it has marital relationship consistent with the rule of excluded degrees quite impossible. Some of the Baniya sub-castes count no more than 100 families. They are so inter-elated they find it extremely difficult to marry within their castes without transgressing the rules of consanguinity.

It is noteworthy that small excuses suffice to bring about this splitting of castes into sub-castes. Castes become sub-divided into sub-castes by reason of change of location, change of occupation, change in social practices, change due to pollution, changes due to increased prosperity, changes due to quarrel and changes due to change of religion. Mr. Blunt has given many instances to illustrate this tendency among the Hindus. There is no space to reproduce all except one which shows how ordinary quarrels lead to the splitting one caste into sub-castes. As stated by Mr. Blunt[3]:—

" In Lucknow there was a sub-caste of Khatika consisting of three ghols or groups, known as Manikpur, Jaiswala and Dalman. They inter-married, ate together, and met together in panchayat under the presidency of their Chaudharis or headmen. Twenty years ago each group had one Chaudhri, but now Jaiswala have three and Manikpur two. The quarrel was as follows. Firstly a woman (her ghol is not given) peddled fruit about the streets. The brethren ordered her to desist from the practice, which is derogatory to the caste's dignity; women should only sell in shops. Her husband and she proved contumacious; and finally their own ghol, acting singly, outcaste the man.

The Dalmu ghol, however, dissenting from this action admitted the husband to communion with themselves upon payment of a fine of Rs. 80 in lieu of excommunication. Secondly a man (the ghol, again is not given) was excommunicated by his own ghol, acting alone; and while his case was under trial, the Jaiswala Chaudhri invited him to dinner by mistake. Thereupon, the three ghols, acting in concert, fined the Chaudhri Rs. 30. Lastly, fines had accumulated and it was decided to hold a Katha (sacred recitation). The Dalmu Chaudhri said he preferred to have his share of money; but the Manikpur Chaudhri (who seems to have kept the joint purse) refused, taking up the attitude that there was going to be a Katha to which the Dalmu people could come or not as they liked. The matter at this stage was brought into court; meanwhile the three ghols ceased to inter-rnarry, so that one endogamous sub-caste split into three quarrels, ghol was pitted against ghol.

If in any caste a group should adopt some new or unusual worship of which other members do not approve, one would expect that group to break off and become an endogamous sub-caste. That such sub-castes are uncommon is due to the tolerance about what and

---

3   "The Caste system of Northern India" pp. 51-56.

with whom he eats and whom he marries. We do, however, find that the Mahabhiras and Panchipriya sub-castes amongst Telis, Koris and the Namakshalis amongst Barhais, Bhangis and Kadheras. "

How do these castes behave towards one another. Their guiding principle is ' be separate ', ' do not intermarry ', ' do not inter-dine ' and ' do not touch '. Mr. Blunt1 has well described the situation when he says:

" A Hindu sits down to a meal either alone or with his caste fellows. The women cannot eat with the men; they wait till their lords have finished. So long as the meal or a part of it consists of Kachcha food (as it usually does, since Chapatis appear at most meals), the man must dine with the precautions of a magic ceremony. He sits within a square marked off on the ground (chauka) inside which is the Chulha or cooking place. Should a stranger's shadow fall upon this square, all food cooked within it is polluted and must be thrown away. In camp Hindu servants may be seen, each well apart from the rest, each within his own chauka, cooking his food upon his own mud oven and eating alone. .

" Rules regarding the acceptance of water are on the whole the same as those regarding the acceptance of a pakka food, but with a tendency to greater laxity. The vessel in which the water is contained affects the question. A high caste man will allow a low caste man to fill his lota (drinking vessel) for him; but he will not drink from the lota of that low caste man. Or a high caste man will give anybody (save Untouchables) a drink, by pouring water from his own lota into that of the drinker; all the men employed at stations to supply railway travellers with water are Barhais, Bans, Bharbhunjas, Halwais, Kahars, and Nais; and of course from higher castes still.

Rules regarding smoking are stricter. It is very seldom that a man will smoke with anybody but a caste fellow; the reason, no doubt is that smoking with a man usually involves smoking his pipe, and this involves much closer contact even than eating food which he has prepared. So stringent is this rule, indeed, that the fact that

Jats, Ahirs, and Gujars will smoke together has beer regarded as a ground for supposing that they are closely akin. Some castes, the Kayastha for instance, differentiates between smoking in a fashion in which the hands are closed round the pipe and the smoke is drawn in without putting the stem actually in the mouth—and smoking in the usual way. Little need be said on the subject of vessels. There are rules laying down what sort of vessels should be made, but they are rather religious than social. Hindus must use brass or alloy (although the use of alloy is hedged about by numerous and minute injunctions, and if such vessels become impure, the only remedy is to get them remoulded). The risk of pollution makes it imperative for every man to have a few vessels of his own. The minimum consists of a lota (drinking vessel), batna (cooking pot), and thali (dish). Better class folk add a Katora (spoon) and Gagra (Water pot). For feasts, the brotherhood usually keep a set of larger vessels of all kinds,which they end to the host; these are bought with the proceeds of fines, and are common property. "[4]

What fraternity can there be in a social order based upon such sentiments? Far from working in a spirit of fraternity the mutual relations of the castes are fratricidal. Class-consciousness, class struggle and class wars are supposed to be ideologies, which came into vogue from the writings of Karl Marx. This is a complete mistake. India is the land, which has experienced class-consciousness, class struggle. Indeed, India is the land where there has been fought a class war between Brahmans and Kshatriyas[5] which lasted for several generations and which was fought so hard and with such virulence that it turned but to be a war of extermination.

---

4   In the Northern India the bar to eating together applies only when the food is kachcha food. In Southern India the bar is complete and applies even when the food is pucca food. Kachcha food is food cooked in water. Pacca food is food cooked in ghee

5   See my book 'Who were the Shudras?'

It must not be supposed that the fratricidal spirit has given place to a spirit of fraternity. The same spirit of separation marks the Hindu social order today as may be seen from what follows:

Each class claims a separate origin. Some claim origin from a Rishi or from a hero. But in each case it is a different Rishi or a different hero having nothing to do with the Rishis and heroes claimed by other castes as their progenitors. Each caste is engaged in nothing but establishing for itself a status superior to that of another caste. This is best illustrated by rules of hyper commonality and rules of hyper gamy. As pointed out by Mr. Blunt[6]:

" It is essential to realise that in respect of the cooking taboo, the criterion is the caste of the person who cooks the food, not the caste of the person who offers it. It follows, therefore, that a high caste Hindu can eat the food of a man of any caste, however low, if his host possesses a cook of suitable caste. And that is why so many cooks are Brahmins. The Hindu draws a distinction between kachcha food, which is cooked in water and pucca food, which is cooked with ghee (clarified butter). This distinction depends on the principle that ghee, like all the products of the sacred cow, protects from impurity, and since such protection is the object of all food taboos, this convenient fiction enables the Hindu to be less particular in the case of pucca food than of kachcha food, and to relax his restrictions accordingly: Speaking of hyper gamy, Mr. Blunt[7] says:—

"The custom of hyper gamy introduces an important modification into the marriage laws of many castes. Where it prevails, the exogamous groups are classified according to their social position; and whilst a group of highest rank will take brides from it, it will not give brides to a group of lower rank. The law is found most highly developed amongst Rajputs but it is observed by many other castes. . . .. Indeed amongst all Hindus there is probably a tendency towards hyper-gamy. "

---

6   1' The Caste system of Northern India ' pp. 89-90.
7   Ibid. ' The Caste system of Northern India '.

What is it that has behind these rules regarding hyper-communality and hypergamy?

Nothing else but the spirit of high and low. All castes are infested with that spirit and there is no caste, which is free from it. The Hindu social order is a ladder of castes placed one above the other together representing an ascending scale of hatred and a descending scale of contempt.

This spirit has exhibited itself in the proverbs coined by one caste with the object of lampooning another caste. It has given rise even to literature by authors of low castes suggesting filthy origin of the so-called high caste. The Sahyadrikhand is the best illustration of it. It is one of the Puranas, which form part of the Hindu sacred literature. It is a Purana of a style quite different from the traditional puranas. It deals with the origin of the different castes. In doing so, it assigns noble origin to other castes while it assigns to the Brahmin caste the filthiest origin.

Does the Hindu social order recognise equality?

The answer must be in the negative. That men are born equal is a doctrine, which is repugnant to the Hindu social order. In the spiritual sense it treats the doctrine as false. According to the Hindu social order though it is true that men are the children of Prajapati the Creator of the Universe, they are not equal on that account. For, they were created from the different parts of the body of Prajapati. The Brahmins were created from the mouth, the Kshatriyas from the arms, the Vaishyas from his thighs and Shudras from his feet. The limbs from which they were created being of unequal value the men thus created are as unequal. In the biological sense, the Hindu social order does not bother to examine whether the doctrine is founded in a fact. If it was not a fact, i.e., men were not equal in their character and natural endowments of character and intelligence so much the better. On the other hand, if it was a fact, i.e., men were equal in character and natural endowments, so much the worse for the doctrine. The Hindu social order is indifferent to the doctrine as a fact. It is equally indifferent to it as an ethical principle. It refuses to recognise that men no matter how profoundly they differ as individuals in capacity and character, are equally entitled as human beings to consideration and respect and that the well-being of a society is likely to be increased if it so plans its organisation that, whether their powers are great or small, all its members may be equally enabled to make the best of such powers as they possess. It will not allow equality of circumstances, institutions and manner of life. It is against equality temper.

III

If the Hindu social order is not based on equality and fraternity, what are the principles on which it is based? There is only one answer to this question. Though few will be able to realise what they are, there is no doubt as to their nature and effect on Hindu society. The Hindu social order is reared on three principles. Among these the first and foremost is the principle of graded inequality.

That the principle of graded inequality is a fundamental principle is beyond controversy. The four classes are not on horizontal plane, different but equal. They are on vertical plane. Not only different but unequal in status, one standing above the other. In the scheme of Manu, the Brahmin is placed at the first in rank. Below him is the Kshatriya. Below the Kshatriya is the Vaishya. Below Vaishya is the Shudra and below Shudra is the Ati-shudra or the Untouchable. This order of precedence among the classes is not merely conventional. It is spiritual, moral and legal. There is no sphere of life, which is not regulated by this principle of graded inequality.

One can substantiate this by numerous illustrations from the Manu Smriti. I will take four illustrations to prove the point. They will be the law of slavery, law of marriage, law of punishment and law of Samskaras and law of Sanyas. The Hindu law recognised slavery as a legal institution. Manu Smriti recognised seven kinds of slaves. Narada Smriti recognised fifteen kinds of slaves. These differences as to the number of slaves and the classes under which they fall is a matter of no importance. What is important is to know who could enslave whom. On this point, the following citations from the Narada Smriti and the Yajnavalkya Smriti are revealing:

Narada Smriti : V. 39. " In the inverse order of four castes slavery is not ordained except where a man violates the duties peculiar to his caste. Slavery (in that respect) is analogous to the condition of a wife. "

Yajnavalkya Smriti: XVI. 183 (2). "Slavery is in the descending order of the Varnas and not in the ascending order. "

Recognition of slavery was bad enough. But if the rule of slavery had been left free to take its own course it would have had at least one beneficial effect. It would have been a levelling force. The foundation of caste would have been destroyed. For under it, a Brahmin might have become the slave of the Untouchables and the Untouchables would have become the masters of the Brahmin. But it was seen that unfettered slavery was a principle and an attempt was made to nullify it. Manu and his successors therefore while recognising slavery ordain that it shall not be recognised in its inverse order to the Varna system. That means that a Brahmin may become the slave of another Brahmin. But he shall not be the slave of a person of another Varna, i.e., of the Kshatriya, Vaishya, Shudra, or Ati-Shudra. On the other hand, a Brahmin may hold as his slave anyone belonging to the four Varnas. A Kshatriya can have a Kshatriya, Vaishya, Shudra and Ati-Shudra as his slaves but not one who is a Brahmin. A Vaishya can have a Vaishya, Shudra and Ati-Shudra as his slaves but not one who is a Brahmin or a Kshatriya. A Shudra can hold a Shudra and an Ati-Shudra, as his slaves but not one who is a Brahmin, Kshatriya or a Vaishya. Ati-Shudra can hold an Ati-Shudra as his slave but not one who is a Brahmin, Kshatriya, Vaishya or Shudra.

Another illustration of this principle of graded inequality is to be found in the Laws of marriage. Manu says :—

III. 12. " For the first marriage of the twice-born classes, a woman of the same class is recommended but for such as are impelled by inclination to marry again, women in the direct order of the classes are to be preferred. "

III. 13. " A Shudra woman only must be the wife of a Shudra; she and a Vaishya, of a Vaishya; they two and a Kshatriya of a Kshatriya; those three and a Brahmani of a Brahmin. " Manu is of course opposed to inter-marriage. His injunction is for each class to marry within his class. But he does recognise marriage outside the defined class. Here again, he is particularly careful not to allow inter-marriage to do harm to his principle of inequality among classes. Like slavery he permits inter-marriage but not in the inverse order. A Brahmin when marrying outside his class may marry any woman from any of the classes below him. A Kshatriya is free to marry a woman from the two classes next below him, namely, the Vaishya and Shudra but must not marry a woman from the Brahmin class which is above him. A Vaishya is free to marry a woman from the Shudra class which is next below him. But he cannot marry a woman from the Brahmin and the Kshatriya class which are above him.

The third illustration is to be found in the Rule of Law as enunciated by Manu. First as to treatment to be given to witnesses. According to Manu, they are to be sworn as follows:

VIII. 87. " In the forenoon let the judge, being purified, severally call on the twice-born, being purified also, to declare the truth, in the presence of some image, a symbol of the divinity and of Brahmins, while the witnesses turn their faces either to the north or to the east. "

VIII. 88. " To a Brahmin he must begin with saying ' ' Declare '; to a Kshatriya, with saying 'Declare the truth'; to a Vaishya admonishing him by mentioning his kine, grain or gold; to a Shudra, threatening him with the guilt of every crime that causes loss of caste. "

Take the punishment of offences as laid down by Manu. To begin with, punishment for defamation:

VIII. 267. "A soldier, defaming a priest, shall be fined a hundred panas; merchant thus offending, a hundred and fifty, or two hundred; but for such an offence a mechanic or servile man shall be whipped. "

VIII. 268. " A priest shall be fined fifty if he slanders a soldier; twenty-five if a merchant and twelve if he slanders a man of the servile class. "

Take the offence of insults. The punishment prescribed by Manu is as follows:

VIII. 270. " A Shudra who insults a Dvija with gross invectives, ought to have his tongue slit for he sprang from the lowest part of Brahma. "

VIII. 271. "If he mentions their names and classes with contumely, as if he says, ' Oh Devadatta, thou refuse of Brahmin '; an iron style, ten fingers long, shall be thrust red into his mouth. "

VIII. 272. " Should he, through pride, give instructions to Brahmins concerning their duty; let the king order some hot oil to be dropped into his mouth and his ear. " Punishment for the offence of abuse. Manu says:

VIII. 276. " For mutual abuse by a Brahmin and a Kshatriya, this fine must be imposed by a learned king; the lowest on the Brahmin and the middlemost on the soldier. "

VIII. 277. " A Vaishya and a Shudra must be punished exactly in the same manner according to their respective castes, except the slitting of the tongue of the Shudras. This is the fixed rule of punishment. " Punishment for the offence of assault. Manu propounds:

VIII. 279. " With whatever limb a Shudra shall assault or hurt a Dvija that limb of his shall be cut off, this is in accordance of Manu. " Punishment for the offence of arrogance. According to Manu:

VIII. 281. " A Shudra who shall insolently place himself on the same seat with a man of high caste, shall either be branded on his hip and be banished or the King shall cause a gash to be made on his buttock. "

VIII. 282. " Should he spit on him through pride, the king shall order both his lips to be gashed; should he urine on him, his penis; should he break wind against him, his anus. "

VIII. 283. "If he seizes the Brahmin by the locks or likewise if he takes him by the feet, let the king unhesitatingly cut off his hands, or by the beard, or by the throat or by the scrotum. " Punishment for the offence of adultery says Manu.

VIII. 359. " A man who is not a Brahmin who commits actual adultery ought to suffer death; for the wives, indeed of all the four classes must ever be most especially guarded. "

VIII. 366. "A Shudra who makes love to a damsel of high birth, ought to be punished corporally; but he who addresses a maid of equal rank, shall give the nuptial present and marry her, if her father desires it. "

VIII. 374. " A Shudra having an adulterous connection with a woman of a twice-born class, whether guarded at home or unguarded shall thus be punished in the following manner; if she was unguarded, he shall lose the part offending and all his property; if guarded everything even his life. "

VIII. 375. " For adultery with a guarded Brahmin a Vaishya shall forfeit all his wealth after imprisonment for a year; a Kshatriya shall be fined a thousand panas, and he be shaved with the urine of an ass. "

VIII. 376. "But if a Vaishya or Kshatriya commits adultery with an unguarded Brahmin, the king shall only fine the Vaishya five hundred panas and the Kshatriya a thousand. "

VIII. 377. " But even these two however, it they commit that offence with a Brahmani not only guarded but the wife of an • eminent man, shall be punished like a Shudra or be burned in a fire of dry grass or reeds. "

VIII. 382. " If a Vaishya approaches a guarded female of the Kshatriya or a Kshatriya a guarded Vaishya woman, they both deserve the same punishment as in the case of an unguarded Brahmin female. "

VIII. 383. " But a Brahmin, who shall commit adultery with a guarded woman of those two classes, must be fined a thousand panas, and for the offending with a Shudra woman the fine of a thousand panas on a Kshatriya or Vaishya. "

VIII. 384. " For adultery by a Vaishya with a woman of the Kshatriya classes, if guarded, the fine is five hundred; but a Kshatriya for committing adultery on a Vaishya woman must be shaved with urine or pay the fine just mentioned. " How strange is the contrast between Hindu and non-Hindu criminal jurisprudence! How inequality is writ large in Hinduism as seen in its criminal jurisprudence! In a Penal Code charged with the spirit of justice we find two things—-a section dealing with defining the crime and a section prescribing a rational form of punishment for breach of it and a rule that all offenders are liable to the same penalty. In Manu, what do we find? First an irrational system of punishment. The punishment for a crime is inflicted on the origin concerned in the crime such as belly, tongue, nose, eyes, ears, organs of generation etc., as if the offending organ was sentiment having a will for its own and had not been merely a survivor of human being. Second feature of Manu's Penal Code is the inhuman character of the punishment, which has no proportion to the gravity of the offence. But the most striking feature of Manu's Penal Code, which stands out in all its nakedness, is the inequality of punishment for the same offence. Inequality designed not merely to punish the offender but to protect also the dignity and to maintain the baseness of the parties coming to a Court of Law to seek justice; in other words to maintain the social inequality on which his whole scheme is founded.

The principle of graded inequality has been carried into the economic field. " From each according to his ability; to each according to his need " is not the principle of Hindu social order. The principle of the Hindu social order is: " From each according to his need. To each according to his nobility. "[8] Supposing an officer was distributing dole to a famine stricken people. He would be bound to give greater dole to a person of high birth than he would to a person of low birth. Supposing an officer was levying taxation. He would be bound to assess a person of high birth at a lower rate than he would to a person of low birth. The Hindu social order does not recognise equal need, equal work or equal ability as the basis of reward for labour. Its motto is that in regard to the distribution of the good things of life those who are reckoned as the highest must get the most and the pest and those who are classed as the lowest must accept the least the worst.

Nothing more seems to be necessary to prove that the Hindu social order is based on the principle of graded inequality. It pervades all departments of social life. Every side of social life is protected against the danger of equality.

The second principle on which the Hindu social order is founded is that of fixate of occupations for each class and continuance thereof by heredity. This is what Manu says about occupations of the four classes.

"1. 87. But in order to protect this universe, He, the most resplendent one, assigned separate (duties and) occupations, to those who sprang from his mouth, arms, thighs and feet.

1. 88. To Brahmanas he assigned teaching and studying (the Veda) sacrificing for their own benefit and for others, giving and accepting (of alms).

1. 89. The Kshatriya he commanded to protect the people, to bestow gifts to offer sacrifices to study (the Veda) and to abstain from attaching himself to sensual pleasures. "

---

8   The illustrations given above are not merely drawn from imagination. They are acts of history. The differentiation between high and low was recognised by law in the time of the Peshwas. The differentiation about dole exists even now in the Bombay Presidency and was defended by a Congress Minister. These Remarks are not applicable today—Editors.

" I. 90. The Vaishya to tend cattle to bestow gifts to offer sacrifices to study (the Veda) and to abstain from attaching himself to sensual pleasures. "

I. 91. One occupation only the Lord prescribed to the Shudra, to serve meekly even these (other) three castes. " These rules regarding the occupations of the different classes are further amplified by Manu as will be seen from the following citations from his Smriti:

" I. 88. To Brahmans he (Swayambhu Manu) assigned the duties of reading the Veda, of teaching it, of sacrificing, of assisting others to sacrifice, of giving alms if they be rich, and if indigent of receiving of gifts.

I. 89. To defend the people, to give alms, to sacrifice, to read the Veda, to shun the allurements of sensual gratification, are in a few words, the duties of a Kshatriya.

I. 90. To keep herds of cattle, to bestow largeness, to sacrifice, to read the scriptures, to carry on trade, to lend at interest, and to cultivate land are prescribed or permitted to a Vaishya.

I. 91. One principal duty the supreme Ruler assigns to a Shudra; namely, to serve the before mentioned classes, without depreciating their worth.

X. 74. Let such Brahmans as are intent on the means of attaining the supreme godhead, and firm in their own duties, completely perform in order, the six following acts.

X. 75. Reading the Vedas, the teaching others to read them, sacrificing, and assisting others to sacrifice, giving to the poor if themselves have enough, and accepting gifts from the virtuous if themselves are poor, are the six prescribed acts of the firstborn class. "

"X. 76. But, among those six acts of a Brahman three are his means of subsistence; assisting to sacrifice, teaching the Vedas and receiving gifts from a pure handed giver.

X. 77. Three acts of duty cease with the Brahman and belong not to the Kshatriya, teaching the Vedas, officiating at a sacrifice and thirdly receiving presents.

X. 78. Those three are also (by the fixed rule of law) forbidden to the Vaishya since Manu, the Lord of all men, prescribed not those acts to the two classes, military and commercial.

X. 79. The means of subsistence peculiar to the Kshatriya are bearing arms, either held for striking or missile; to the Vaishya, merchandise, attending on cattle, and agriculture; but with a view to the next life, the duties of both are alms giving, reading and sacrificing. "

Every member must follow the trade assigned to the class to which he belongs. It leaves no scope for individual choice, individual inclination. An individual under the Hindu social order is bound to the profession of his ancestor. It is an inexorable law from which he cannot escape.

The principle does not stop with fixate of occupation. It grades the several occupations in terms of respectability. This is what Manu says:—

" X. 80. Among the several occupations for gaining a livelihood the most commendable respectively for the Brahmans, Kshatriyas and the Vaishyas are the teaching of the Vedas, defending the people and trade.

The third principle on which the Hindu social order is founded is the fixation of people within their respective classes. There is nothing strange or peculiar in the fact that the Hindu social order recognises classes. There are classes everywhere and no society is without them. Families, cliques, clubs, political parties, may communities, gangs engaged in criminal conspiracies, business corporations which prey upon the public are to be found in all societies in all parts of the world. Even a free social order will not be able to get rid of the classes. What a free social order aims to do is to prevent isolation and exclusiveness being regarded by the classes as an ideal to be followed. For so long as the classes do not practise isolation and exclusiveness they are only non-social in their relations towards one another. Isolation and exclusiveness make them anti-social and inimical towards one another. Isolation makes for rigidity of class consciousness, for institutionalising social life and for the dominance of selfish ideals within the classes. Isolation makes life static, continues the separation into a privileged and underprivileged, masters and servants.

Not so much the existence of classes as the spirit of isolation and exclusiveness which is inimical with a free social order. What a free social order endeavours to do is to maintain all channels of social endowment. This is possible only when the classes are free to share in an extensive number of common interests, undertakings and expenses, have a large number of values in common, when there is a free play back and forth, when they have an equable opportunity to receive and to take from others. Such social contacts must and does dissolve custom, makes for an alert and expanding mental life and not only occasion but also demand reconstruction of mental attitudes. What is striking about the Hindu social orders is its ban on free inter-change and inter-course between different classes of Hindu society. There is a bar against inter-dining and inter-marriage. But Manu goes to the length of interdicting ordinary social intercourse. Says Manu:

IV. 244. " He, who seeks to preserve an exalted rank, must constantly form connections with the highest and best families, but avoid the worst and the meanest.

IV. 245. Since a priest, who connects himself with the best and the highest of men, avoiding the lowest and worst, attains eminence ; but sinks by an opposite conduct, to the class of the servile.

IV. 79. Not let him tarry even under the shade of the same tree with outcaste for the great crimes, nor with Chindalas, nor with Puccasas, nor with idiots, nor with man proud of wealth, nor with \\ashcrmcn and other vile persons, nor with Artyevasins.'" The Hindu social order is opposed to fraternity, t does not admit the principle of equality. Far from recognising equality it makes inequality its official doctrine. What about liberty? So far as choice of occupation goes, there is none. Everyone has his occupation determined for him. Only thing left to do is to carry it on. As to freedom of speech it exists. But it exists only for those who are in favour of the social order. The freedom is not the freedom of liberalism which was expressed by Voltaire when i.e. said "I wholly disapprove of what you say and will defend to the death your right to say it. " This is clear from what Manu has to say about Logic and dialectics.

"IV. 29-30. No guest must stay in his house without being honoured according to his ability, with a seat, food, a couch, water, or roots and fruits.

Let him not honour even by greeting heretics, men who follow forbidden occupations, men who live like cats, rogues, logicians (arguing against the Veda) and those who live like herons.

II. 10. But by Sruti (Revelation) is meant the Vedas and by Smriti (tradition) the Institutes of the sacred law ; those two must not be called into question in any matter, since from those two the sacred law shone forth.

II. II. Every twice-born man, who, relying on the Institutes of dialectics, treats with contempt those two sources (of the law), must be cast out by the virtuous as an atheist and a scorner of the Veda.

II. 12. The Veda, the sacred tradition, the customs of virtuous men, and one's own pleasure, they declare to be visibly the fourfold means of defining the sacred law. " The reasons for this are made manifest by Manu who says:

II. 6. "The whole Veda is the (first) source of the sacred law, next the tradition and the virtuous conduct of those who know the (Veda further) also the customs of holy men, and (finally) self- satisfaction:

II. 7. Whatever law has been ordained for any (person) by Manu; that has been fully declared in the Veda; for that (sage was) omniscient. "

In this freedom there is not freedom for dialecticians, no freedom for logicians to criticise the social order which means there is no freedom at all.

What about liberty of action? In the sense of effective choice, there is no room for it in the Hindu social order. The Hindu social order leaves no choice to the individual. It fixes his occupation. It fixes his status. All that remains for the individual to do is to conform him self to these regulations.

The same must be said with regard to political liberty. The Hindu social order does not recognise the necessity of a representative government composed of the representatives chosen by the people. Representative Government rests on the belief that people must be governed by law and law can be made only by the representative of the people. The Hindu social order recognises the first part of this thesis, which says that people must be governed by law. But it denies the second part of the thesis, which says that law can be made only by the representatives chosen by the people. The tenets of the Hindu social order is that the law by which people are to be governed is already made and is to be found in the Vedas. Nobody has a right to add to and subtract from it. That being so. a representative assembly of the people is unnecessary. Political liberty which is liberty to frame laws and to make and unmake Government is futility for which there is no place in the Hindu social order.

To sum up, the Hindu social order is an order based on classes and not on individual. It is an order in which classes are graded one above the other. It is an order in which the status and functions of the classes are determined and fixed. The Hindu social order is a rigid order. No matter what changes take place in the relative position of an individual his social status as a member of the class he is born in relation to another person belonging to another class shall in no way be affected. The first shall never become the last. The last shall never become the first.

The Hindu Social Order: Its Unique Features

So far the discussions were confined to describing the essentials of the Hindu social order. Besides its essentials, the Hindu social order has some unique features. These unique features are as important as the essentials. No study of the Hindu social order, which does not make any reference to them, can be regarded as complete or accurate.

What are these special features? The special features of the Hindu social order are three in number. Of these three, the most striking is the worship of the superman. In this respect the Hindu social order is nothing but Nietzsche's Gospel put in action. Nietzsche himself never claimed any originality for his theory of the superman. He admitted and avowed that he borrowed it from the Manu Smriti. In his treatise, called Anti-Christ this is what Nietzsche said :—

"After all, the question is, to what end are falsehoods perpetrated? The fact that, in Christianity, ' Holy ends are entirely absent, constitutes my objection to the means it employs. Its ends are only bad ends; the poisoning, the calumniation and the denial of life, the contempt of the body, the degradation and self-pollution of man by virtue of the contempt of sin, consequently its means are bad as well. My feelings are quite the reverse when I read the law book of Manu, an incomparably intellectual and superior work, which it would be a sin against the spirit even to mention in the same breath with the Bible. You will guess immediately why it has a genuine philosophy behind it. In it, not merely an evil smelling Jewish distillation of Rabbinism and superstition it gives something to chew even to the most fastidious psychologist. And, not to forget the most important point of all, it is fundamentally different from the very kind of Bible; by means of it the noble classes, the philosophers and the warriors guard and guide the masses; it is replete with noble values, it is filled with a feeling of perfection with saying yea to life, triumphant sense of well-being in regard to itself and to life, the Sun shines upon the whole book. All those things which Christianity smothers with its bottomless vulgarity; procreation, women, marriages are here treated with earnestness, with reverence, with love and confidence. How can one possibly place in the hands of children and women, a book that contains those vile words; ' to avoid fornication let every man have his wife, let every woman have her own husband. . . . It is better to marry than to burn. And is it decent to be a Christian so long as the very origin of man is Christianised that is to say, befouled, by the idea of the Immaculate Conception. "

Nietzsche never got any respectful or serious hearing in his own country. In his own words, he was ' sometimes defied as the philosopher of the aristocracy and squiarchy, sometimes hooted at, sometimes pitied and sometimes boycotted as an inhuman being. ' Nietzsche's philosophy had become identified with will to power, will to violence and denial of spiritual values, sacrifice, servility to and debasement of the common man in the interest of the superman. His philosophy with these high spots had created a feeling of loathsomeness and horror in the minds of the people of his own generation. He was utterly neglected if not shunned and Nietzsche himself took comfort by placing himself among the ' posthumous men '. He foresaw for himself a remote public, centuries after his own time to appreciate him. Here too Nietzsche was destined to be disappointed. Instead of there being any appreciation of his philosophy the lapse of time has only augmented the horror and loathing which people of his generation felt for Nietzsche. Having regarded to the vile nature of Nietzsche's philosophy some people may not be ready to believe that the Hindu social order is based on the worship of the Superman.

Let the Manu Smriti speak on this point. This is what Manu says with regard to the position of the Brahmin in the Hindu social order.

I. 93. " As the Brahmana sprang from Prajapati's (i.e. God's) mouth, as he was first-born, and as he possesses the Veda, he is by right the Lord of this whole creation. "

I. 94. " For the self-existent (Swayambhu) i.e. God having performed austerities, produced him first from his own mouth, in order that the offerings might be conveyed to the Gods and Manes and that this universe might be preserved. "

I. 95. " What created being can surpass him, through whose mouth the Gods continually consume the sacrificial viands and the Manes the offerings to the dead. "

I. 96. " Of created beings the most excellent are said to be those which are animated, of the animated those who subsist by intelligence; of the intelligent mankind, and of the men the Brahmans. "

Besides the reason given by Manu the Brahman is first in rank because he was produced by God from his mouth, in order that the offerings might be conveyed to the Gods and manes, Manu gives another reason for the supremacy of the Brahman. He says:

I. 98. " The very birth of a Brahmana is an eternal incarnation of the sacred law (Veda) for he is born to (fulfil) the sacred law, and becomes one with Brahman (God.)"

I. 99. " A Brahmana coming into existence, is born as the highest on earth, the Lord of all created beings, for the protection of the treasury of the law. " Manu concludes by saying that :

I. 101. "The Brahmana eats but his own food, wears but his own apparel, bestows but his own in alms ; other mortals subsist through the benevolence of the Brahmana. " Because according to Manu :

I. 100. "Whatever exists in the world is the property of the Brahmana ; on account of the excellence of his origin the Brahmana is, indeed, entitled to it all. "

Being a deity the Brahman is above law and above the king. Manu directs :

VII. 37. "Let the king, rising early in the morning, worship Brahmanas who are well-versed in the threefold sacred science and learned (in polity) and follow their advice. "

VII. 38. " Let him daily worship aged Brahmans who know the Veda and are pure....." Finally Manu says:

XI. 35. " The Brahman is (hereby) declared to be the creator (of the world), the punisher, the teacher, (and hence) a benefactor (of all created beings) to him let no man say anything unpropitious, nor use any harsh words." Manu ordains that:

X. 3. " From priority of birth, from superiority of origin, from a more exact knowledge of scripture, and from a distinction in the sacrificial thread, the Brahman is the lord of all classes. " The Brahmin or the Superman of the Hindu social order was entitled to certain privileges. In the first place, he could not be hanged even though he might be guilty of murder.[9] Manu says:

VIII. 379. " Ignominious tonsure is ordained, instead of capital punishment, for a Brahmin adulterer where the punishment of other classes may extend to loss of life. "

VIII. 380. "Never shall the king slay a Brahmin, though convicted of all possible crimes; let him banish the offender from his realm, but with all his property secure, and his body unhurt. "

XI. 127. " For a Brahmin killing intentionally a virtuous man of the Kshatriya class, the penance must be a fourth part of that ordained for killing a priest; for killing a Vaishya, only an eighth; for killing a Shudra, who had been constant in discharging his duties a sixteenth part. "

XI. 128. "But, if a Brahmin kills a Kshatriya without malice, he must, after a full performance of his religious rites give the priests one bull together with a thousand cows. "

---

9   This immunity was continued by the British Government up to 1837. It was in 1837 the Penal Law was amended whereby the Brahman for the first time became liable to capita punishment for murder. The immunity still exists in Indian States. In Travancore the Dewan who is a Brahmin adopted an ingenious method of meeting public criticism of this continuance of this privilege. Instead of hanging the Brahmins he abolished capital punishment altogether.

XI. 129. "Or he may perform for three years the penance for slaying a Brahmin, mortifying his organs of sensation and action, letting his hair grow long, and living remote from the town, with the root of a tree for his mansion. "

XI. 130. " If he kills without malice a Vaishya, who had a good moral character, he may perform the same penance for one year, or give the priests a hundred cows and a bull. "

XI. 131. " For six months must he perform this whole penance, if without intention he kills a Shudra, or he may give ten white cows and a bull to the priests. "

VIII. 381. "No greater crime is known on earth than slaying a Brahmin; and the king, therefore must not even form in his mind an idea of killing a priest. "

VIII. 126. " Let the king having considered and ascertained the frequency of a similar offence, the place and time, the ability of the criminal to pay or suffer and the crime itself, cause punishment to fall on those alone, who deserve it. "

VIII. 124. "Manu, son of the self-existent, has named ten places of punishment, which are appropriated to the three lower classes. but a Brahmin must depart from the realm unhurt in any one of them. "

The Brahmin has been given by the Manu Smriti other privileges. In the matter of marriage in addition to his marrying a woman of his own class he is entitled[10] to enter into wedlock with a woman of any of the classes lower to him without being bound to the woman by the tie of marriage or conferring upon the children the right to his status or to his property.

He had the power to punish his wrongdoer without resort to court[11].

He could take the property of the common man (the Shudra) without compensation and without reference to court if the same

---

10 Manu III. 12-13 This privilege is recognised by Courts in India

11 Manu XI. 31—This privilege has been abolished,

was necessary for the performance of his religious duties[12]. If he discovers a hidden treasure he was free to appropriate the whole[13] of it without giving the usual share to the king ' since he was the lord of all ' and was entitled to claim half[14] if it was discovered by another. He was entitled to whole amount accumulated from legal fines from a king whose death was due to some incurable disease[15]. He was exempt from taxation[16]. He was entitled to compel the king to provide for his daily food and to see that he did not starve[17]. His property was free from the law of escheat[18].

The superman of the Hindu Social order is not bound by the rules as to occupation if he is in distress. Manu says:—

X. 81. "Yet a Brahman, unable to subsist by his duties just mentioned, may live by the duty of a soldier; for that is the next in rank. "

X. 82. " If it be asked, how he must live, should he be unable to get a subsistence by either of those employment; the answer is, he may subsist as a mercantile man, applying himself in person to tillage and attendance on cattle. "

X. 83. " But a Brahman and a Kshatriya, obliged to subsist by the acts of a Vaishya, must avoid with care, if they can live by keeping herds, the business of tillage, which gives great pain to sentient creatures, and is dependent on the labour of others, as bulls and so forth. "

X. 84. " Some are of opinion, that agriculture is excellent but it is a mode of subsistence which the benevolent greatly blame, for the iron mouthed pieces of wood not only wound the earth, but the creatures dwelling in it. "

---

12 Manu XI. 32.—This privilege no longer exsists.

13 Manu VIII. 37.

14 Manu VIII. 38.

15 Manu IX. 323.

16 6 Manu VII. 133.

17 Manu VII. 134.

18 Manu IX. 189.

X. 85. " If, through want of a virtuous livelihood, they cannot follow laudable occupations, they may then gain a competence of wealth by selling commodities usually sold by merchants, avoiding what ought to be avoided. "

X. 102. " The Brahman, having fallen into distress, may receive gifts from any person whatever; for by no sacred rule can it be shown, that absolute purity can be sullied. "

X. 103. "From interpreting the Veda, from officiating at sacrifices or from taking presents, though in modes generally disapproved, no sin is committed by priests in distress; for they are as pure as fire or water. "

The privileges of the superman are not at all counterbalanced by an obligation towards the common man. Indeed the superman has no duty towards the common man.

He is not bound to do charity for the uplift of the Common man. On the other hand, to receive charity is the monopoly of the Superman. For any other person to receive charity is a sin. To the Common man (Shudra) who is born to serve the Superman man, the Superman is not at all required to be a good employer and is not bound to keep him well-fed, well clothed and well-housed. His obligations in this behalf as laid down by Manu are stated below:

X. 124. "They must allot to him (Shudra) out of their own family property a suitable maintenance after considering his ability, his industry and the number of those whom he is bound to support. "

X. 125. "The remnants of their food must be given to him, as well as their old clothes, the refuse of their grain, and their old household furniture.

The rise of the Common man is antagonistic to the supremacy of the Superman. In order to keep the Superman satisfied, happy and secure the Hindu social order takes special care to keep the Common man in a state of perpetual degradation.

Manu insists on the Shudra doing nothing but service: X. 122. "But let a Shudra serve Brahmans." X. 121. "If a Shudra unable to subsist by serving Brahmanas seeks a livelihood, he may serve Kshatriyas, or he may also seek to maintain himself by attending on a wealthy Vaishya. "

I. 91. "One occupation only the lord prescribed to the Shudra, to serve meekly even these other three castes. " And why? Manu does not hesitate to give the reason. He says:

X. 129. "No superfluous collection of wealth must be made by a Shudra, even though he has power to make it, since a servile man, who has amassed riches, becomes proud, and, by his insolence or neglect, gives pain even to Brahmanas."

The common man is not permitted to acquire learning. The following are the injunctions of Manu:

I. 88. "To the Brahmanas he (the creator) assigned teaching and studying the Veda. "

I. 89. " The Kshatriya he (the creator) commanded to study the Veda. "

II. 116. " He who shall acquire knowledge of the Veda without the assent of his preceptor incurs the guilt of stealing the scripture, and shall sink to the region of torment. "

IV. 99. " He (the twice-born) must never read the Veda. . . . in the presence of the Shudras. "

IX. 18. " Women have no business with the text of the Veda. " IX. 199. "A twice-born man who has... (improperly) divulged the Veda (ie., to Shudras and women) commits sin, atones for his offence, if he subsists a year on barley. " In those texts there are embodied three distinct propositions. The Brahmins, Kshatriyas and Vaishyas can study the Vedas. Of these the Brahmans alone have the right to teach the Vedas But in the case of the Shudra he has not only to study the Vedas but he should not be allowed to hear it read.

The successors of Manu made the disability of the Shudra in the matter of the study of the Veda into an offence involving dire penalties. For instance, Gautama says:

III. 4. "If the Shudra intentionally listens for committing to memory the Veda, then his ears should be filled with (molten) lead and lac; if he utters the Veda, then his tongue should be cut off; if he has mastered the Veda his body should be cut to pieces. " To the same effect is Katyayana.

The common man (Shudra) is not allowed the benefit of the sacrament of initiation. It is the second birth that helps towards the moral and material advancement of the individual.

The common man is denied the right to have a name conveying dignity. Manu says:

II. 30. " Let the father perform or cause to be performed the Namadheya (the rite of name of the child), on the tenth or twelfth (day after birth), or on a lucky lunar day in a lucky muhurth under an auspicious constellation.

II. 31. "Let (the first part of) a Brahman's name (denote something) auspicious, a Kshatriya name be connected with power, and a Vaishya with wealth, but a Shudra's (express something) contemptible. "

II. 32. " (The second part of) a Brahman's name shall be a word implying happiness, of a Kshatriya (a word) implying protection, of a Vaishya (a term) expressive of thriving and of a Shudra's (an expression) denoting a service. "

The Superman will not tolerate the Shudra to have the comfort of a high-sounding name. He must be contemptible both in fact and in name.

A Hindu's life is divided into periods. The first period is called Brahmacharya, the stage of a student. The second period is called Grahasthashram, the stage of married life. The third period is called Vanasprastha, the stage of detachment from worldly life. The fourth period is called Sanyasa which is complete severance from the affairs of the world which is tantamount to civil death. The common man is denied the right of becoming a Sanyasi. It is difficult to understand why. Obviously for the benefit of the Superman. A Shudra by becoming a Sanyasi ceases to render service to Superman. A Shudra by becoming a Sanyasi reaches God or Brahma which is an invasion of the privileges of the Superman.

The citations from Manu prove that the Hindu social order is openly and avowedly devised and intended for the good of the Superman. In it everything is ordained for the Superman. The Superman is the Brahmin and the common man is the Shudra. The Superman has rights and no duties. Everything is at the disposal of the Superman, everything must be ascribed in the interests of the Superman. The counterpart of the same feature is the degradation of the common man. As against the Superman the common man has no right to life, liberty, property or pursuit of happiness. He must be ready to sacrifice everything for the sustenance of the life and dignity of the Superman. The Hindu social order prescribes that such sacrifice should be made willingly by the common man. Indeed, it inculcates that the common man should respond to such call for sacrifice in the interest of the Superman as his supreme duty.

Can there be any doubt that Zarathustra is a new name for Manu and that ' Thus spoke Zarathustra ' is a new edition of the Manu Smriti?

If there is any difference between Manu and Nietzsche, it lies in this. Nietzsche was genuinely interested in creating a new race of men which will be race of Superman as compared with the existing race of men. Manu, on the other hand, was interested in maintaining the privilege of a class who had come to arrogate to itself the claim of being Superman. Nietzsche's Supermen were Supermen by reason of their worth. Nietzsche was a genuine distinterested philosopher. Manu, on the contrary, was a hireling engaged to propound a philosophy which served the interests of a class, born in a group and whose title to being Superman was not to be lost even if they lost their virtue. Compare the following texts from Manu.[19]

X. 81. "Yet, a Brahmin, unable to subsist by his duties just mentioned, may live by the duty of a soldier; for that is the next rank. "

X. 82. " If it be asked, how he must live, should he be unable to get a subsistence by either of those employment; the answer is, he may subsist as a mercantile man, applying himself to tillage and an attendance on cattle. " Manu adds:

IX. 317. "A Brahmin, be he ignorant or learned, is a great divinity, just as the fire, whether carried forth (for the performance of a burnt oblation) or not carried forth, is a great divinity. "

IX. 319. "Thus, though the Brahmins employ themselves in all (sorts) of mean occupation, they must be honoured in every way; (for each of) them is a very great deity. "

Nietzsche's praise of the Manu Smriti is undeserved. For when he says that according to its scheme " the noble classes, the philosophers and the warriors guard and guide the masses ", he is either making a positively untrue statement or that he has not read it correctly. Under the Manu Smriti the superman has rights against the common man but he has no duties towards the common man.

Manu's degraded and degenerate philosophy of Superman as compared with that of Nietzsche is therefore far more odious and loathsome than the philosophy of Nietzsche. Such is the social order which the Hindus regard as a pearl without price and which Mr. Gandhi is proud to offer as a gift from the Hindus to the world.

Another special feature of the Hindu social order relates to the technique devised for its preservation. The technique is twofold.

---

19 The correct description of the Brahmin would be the Super-most Superman. For below him and above the common man there are the Kshatriyas and the Vaishyas. But since the Kshatriyas and the Vaishyas are only superiors and not supermen it is unnecessary to change the nomenclature.

The first technique is to place the responsibility of upholding and maintaining the social order upon the shoulders of the King. Manu does this in quite express terms.

VIII. 410. " The King should order each man of the mercantile class to practise trade or money-lending or agriculture and attendance on cattle; and each man of the servile class to act in the service of the twice-born. "

VIII. 418. "With vigilant care should the King exert himself in compelling merchants and mechanics to perform their respective duties; for, when such men swerve from their duty they throw this world into confusion. "

Manu does not stop with the mere enunciation of the duty of the King in this behalf. He wants to ensure that the King shall at all times perform his duty to maintain and preserve the established order. Manu therefore makes two further provisions. One provision is to make the failure of the King to maintain the established order an offence for which the King became liable for prosecution and punishment like a common felon. This would be clear from the following citations from Manu: —

VIII. 335. " Neither a father, nor a preceptor, nor a friend, nor a mother, nor a wife, nor a son, nor a domestic priest must be left unpunished by the King if they adhere not with firmness to their duty. "

VIII. 336. " Where another man of lower birth would be fined one pana, the King shall be fined a thousand, and he shall give the fine to the priests, or cast it into the river, this is a sacred rule. " The other provision made by Manu against a King who is either negligent or opposed to the established order is to irvest the three classes, Brahmins, Kshatriyas and Vaishyas with a right to rise in armed rebellion against the King.

VIII. 348. " The twice-born may take arms, when their duty is obstructed by force; and when, in some evil time, a disaster has befallen the twice-born classes. "

The Right of rebellion is given to the three higher classes and not to the Shudra. This is very natural. Because it is only the three upper classes who would benefit by the maintenance of this system. But supposing the Kshatriyas joined the king in destroying the system what is to be done? Manu gives the authority to the Brahmins to punish all and particularly the Kshatriyas.

XI. 31. " A priest, who well knows the laws, need not complain to the king of any grievous injury; since, even by his own power, he may chastise those, who injure him. "

XI. 32. " His own power, which depends on himself alone, is mightier than the royal power, which depends on other men; by his own might, therefore, may a Brahmin coerce his foes. "

XI. 33. " He may use without hesitation, the powerful charms revealed to Atharvan, and by him to Angiras; for speech is the weapon of a Brahmin; with that he may destroy his oppressors. "

IX. 320. " Of a military man, who raises his arm violently on all occasions against the priestly class, the priest himself shall be the chastiser; since the soldier originally proceeded from the Brahmin. " How can the Brahmins punish the Kshatriyas unless they can take arms? Manu knows this and therefore allows the Brahmins to arm themselves to punish the Kshatriyas.

XII. 100. "Command of armies, royal authority, power of inflicting punishment, and sovereign dominion over all nations, he only well deserves, who perfectly understands the Veda Sastra i.e., who is a Brahmin. "

The second technique devised for the maintenance and preservation of the established order is quite different from the first. Really speaking, it is this, which constitutes a special feature of the Hindu social order.

In the wake of the preservation of the social order from violent attack it is necessary to bear in mind three considerations. The outbreak of a revolution is conditioned by three factors: (1) the existence of a sense of wrong; (2) capacity to know that one is suffering from a wrong and (3) availability of arms. The second consideration is that there are two ways of dealing with a rebellion. One is to prevent a rebellion from occurring and the other is to suppress it after it has broken out. The third consideration is that whether the prevention of rebellion would be feasible or whether the suppression of rebellion would be the only method opens, would depend upon the rules, which govern the three pre-requisites of rebellion.

When the social order denies opportunity to rise, denies right to education and denies right to use arms, it is in a position to prevent rebellion against the social order. Where on the other hand, a social order allows right to education, and permits the use of arms, it cannot prevent rebellion by those who suffer wrongs. Its only remedy to preserve the social order is by suppression of rebellion by the use of force and violence. The Hindu social order has adopted the first method. It has fixed the social status of the lower orders for all generations to come. Their economic status is also fixed. There being no disparity between the two, there is no possibility of a grievance growing up. It has denied education to the lower orders. The result is that no one is conscious that his low condition is a ground for grievance. If there is any consciousness it is that no one is responsible for the low condition. It is the result of fate. Assuming there is a grievance, assuming there is consciousness of grievance, there cannot be a rebellion by the lower orders against the Hindu social order because the Hindu social order denies the masses the right to use arms. Other social orders such as those of the Muslims or the Nazis, follow the opposite course. They allow equal opportunity to all. They allow freedom to acquire knowledge. They allow the right to bear arms and take upon themselves the odium of suppressing rebellion by force and violence. To deny freedom of opportunity, to deny freedom to acquire knowledge, to deny the right of arms is a most cruel wrong. Its results Manu mutilates and emasculates man. The Hindu social order is not ashamed to do this. It has, however, achieved two things. It has found the most effective, even though it be the most shameless method of preserving the established order.

Secondly, notwithstanding the use of most inhuman means of killing manliness, it has given to the Hindus the reputation of being very humane people. The Nazis had indeed a great deal to learn from the Hindus. If they had adopted the technique of suppressing the masses devised by the Hindus they would have been able to crush the Jews without open cruelty and would have also exhibited themselves as humane masters.

The third special feature of the Hindu social order is that it is a Divine order designed by God himself. As such it is sacred, not open to abrogation, amendment, not even to criticism. For the purpose of removing any doubt that may be lurking in the minds of anybody about the Divine character of the Hindu social order, attention is invited to the following verses from the Bhagvat Gita and the Manu Smriti. Shri Krishna one of the Hindu Gods, whose word is the Bhagvat Gita says:—

IV. 13. "I myself have created the arrangement of the four castes (into Brahmins, Kshatriyas, Vaishyas and Shudras), consistently with the differences in their qualities and actions. It is, I who am the Maker of it. "

XVIII. 41-44. "0, Parantapa! the respective duties of Brahmins (priests), Kshatriyas (warriors), Vaishyas (tradesmen) and Shudras (menials) have been individually fixed with reference to the qualities arising from their inherent natures, that is, from Prakriti. The inherently natural duties of a Brahmin are peace, self-restrain, religious austerities, cleanliness, and quietness, straightforwardness (humanity). Knowledge (that is, spiritual knowledge). Vijnana (that is Imperial knowledge) and Astikya-budhi (that is belief in a future world). The inherently natural duty (karma) of the Kshatriya is bravery, brilliance, courage, intentness, not running away from the battle, generosity, and exercising authority (over subject people) ' goraksya ' (that is the business of keeping cattle), and vanijya (that is, trade) is the inherently natural duty of the Vaishya; and in the same way, service is the inherently natural duty of the Shudra. "

Krishna forbids propaganda against the Hindu social order. He says:—

HI. 26. " As the ignorant act with attachment to action so a wise man wishing to keep the people to their duties, should not shake the convictions of the ignorant who are attached to action, but acting with devotion (himself) should make them apply themselves to all action. . . . A man of perfect knowledge should not shake these men of imperfect knowledge in their convictions. " When the Hindu social order breaks down, Krishna does not want the people to undertake the work of reform. He asks them to leave the task to him. This is evident from the following admonition contained in the Bhagvat Gita. Says Krishna :—

IV. 7-8. "0! Bharata, whenever Righteous less declines and Unrighteousness becomes powerful, then I Myself come to birth. I take birth in different Yugas for protecting the Righteous and destroying the Unrighteous and for establishing Righteousness. " It is not only a special feature of the Hindu social order. It is an extraordinary feature. An examination of consecrations will show that there are instances where society has consecrated inanimate beings and inculcated on the minds of its members the religious belief that they are sacred. There are cases where stones, rivers, trees are made Gods and Goddesses. There are instances where society has consecrated living things and inculcated on the minds of its members the religious belief that they are sacred. But there are no instances where a particular social order has been consecrated by Religion and made sacred. The primitive world had its clan order and its tribal order. But the clan or the tribal order was only a social order and was never consecrated by religion and made sacred and inviolate. The ancient world countries like Egypt, Persia, Rome, Greece, etc., each had its social order in which some were free and some were slaves, some were citizens, some were aliens, some of the race, some of another. This class order again was only a social order and was never consecrated by religion and made sacred and inviolate. The modern world has its order, in some it is Democracy, in some Fascism, in some Nazism and in some Bolshevism. But here again the order is only social order. It is not consecrated by religion and made sacred and inviolate.

Nowhere has society consecrated its occupations—the ways of getting a living. Economic activity has always remained outside the sanctity of religion. Hunting society was not without a religion. But Hunting as an occupation was not consecrated by religion and made sacred. Pastoral society was not without religion. But pastorage was not consecrated by religion and made sacred. Farming as an occupation did not become consecrated by religion and made sacred. Feudalism with its gradations, with its Lords, villains and serfs was a purely social in character. There was nothing sacred about it.

The Hindus are the only people in the world whose social order—the relation of man to man is consecrated by religion and made sacred, eternal and inviolate. The Hindus are the only people in the world whose economic order—the relation of workman to workman, is consecrated by religion and made sacred, eternal and inviolate.

It is not therefore enough to say that the Hindus are a people with a sacred code of religion. So are the Zorastrians, Israelites, Christians and Muslims. All these have sacred codes. They consecrate beliefs and rites and make them sacred. But they do not prescribe, nor do they consecrate a particular form of social structure—the relationship between man and man in a concrete form—and make it sacred inviolate. The Hindus are singular in this respect This is what has given the Hindu social order its abiding strength to defy the ravages of \ time and the onslaught of time.

The orthodox Hindu will accept this as an accurate description of the Hindu social order. It is only the reformer who is likely to demur. He would say that since the advent of the British, this is all a description of a dead past. One need not be perturbed by this view. For it contains a fallacy. It omits to take note of the fact that institutions, which have died as creeds sometimes continue, nevertheless survive as habits. No one can deny that the Hindu social order has become the habit of the Hindus and as such is in full force.

CHAPTER 2

Symbols of Hinduism

Editorial note in the source publication:

There are 37 pages under this title. The chapter seems incomplete. However this relates to the topic No. 7 of the original plan. All these pages are tagged along with the pages of " India and Communism " into One register. We are reproducing the text of this typed copy along with the table of contents written by Dr. Ambedkar. A photo copy of the plan of a proposed book ' Can I be a Hindu ? ' is also reproduced from the original (moth-eaten).—Editors

Is there anything peculiar in the social organisation of the Hindus? An unsophisticated Hindu who is unaware of investigations conducted by scholars will say that there is nothing peculiar, abnormal or unnatural in the organisation of the Hindu society. This is quite natural. People who live their lives in isolation are seldom conscious of the peculiarities of their ways and manners. People have gone on from generation to generation without stopping to give themselves a name. But how does the social organisation of the Hindus strike the outsiders, the non-Hindus? Did it appear to them as normal and natural as it appears to the Hindus?

Megasthenese who came to India as the ambassador of the Greek King Seleukos Nickator to the Court of Chandragupta Maurya some time about the year 305 B.C. did feel that the social organisation of the Hindus was of a very strange sort. Otherwise, he would not have taken such particular care to describe the peculiar feaures of the Hindu social organisation. He has recorded: " The population of India is divided into seven parts. The philosophers are first in rank, but form the smallest class in point of number. Their services are employed privately by persons who wish to offer sacrifices or perform other sacred rites, and also publicly by the kings at what is called the Great Synod, wherein at the beginning of the new year all the philosophers are gathered together before the king at the gates, when any philosopher who may have committed any useful suggestion to writing, or observed any means for improving the crops and the cattle, or for promoting the public interests, declares it publicly. If anyone is detected giving false information thrice, the law condemns him to be silent for the rest of his life, but he who gives sound advice is exempted from paying any taxes or contributions. The second caste consists of the husbandmen, who form the bulk of the population, and are in disposition most mild and gentle. They are exempted from military service, and cultivate their lands undisturbed by fear. They never go to town, either to take part in its tumults, or for any other purpose. It therefore not infrequently happens that at the same time, and in the same part of the country, men may be seen drawn up in array of battle, and fighting at risk of their lives, while other men close at hand are ploughing and digging in perfect security, having these soldiers to protect them. The whole of the land is the property of the king, and the husbandmen till it on condition of receiving one-fourth of the produce.

The third caste consists of herdsmen and hunters, who alone are allowed to hunt, and to keep cattle and to sell draught animals or let them out on hire. In return for clearing the land of wild beasts and fowls, which devour the seeds sown in the fields, they receive an allowance of grain from the king. They lead wandering life and live under tents.

The fourth class, after herdsmen and hunters, consists of those who work at trades, of those who vend wares, and of those who are employed in bodily labour. Some of these pay tribute, and render to the state certain prescribed services. But the armourmakers and shipbuilders receive wages and their victuals from the king, for whom alone they work. The general in command of the army supplies the soldiers with weapons, and the admiral of the fleet lets out ships on hire for the transport both of passengers and merchandise.

The fifth class consists of fighting men, who when not engaged in active service, pass their time in idleness and drinking. They are maintained at the king's expense, and hence they are always ready, when occasion calls, to take the field, for they carry nothing of their own with them but their own bodies.

The sixth class consists of the overseers, to whom is assigned the duty of watching all that goes on, and making reports secretly to the king. Some are entrusted with the inspection of the city, and others with that of the army. The former employs as their coadjutors the courtezans of the city, and the latter the courtezans of the camp. The ablest and most trustworthy men are appointed to fill these offices.

The seventh class consists of the Councillors and assessors of the king. To them belong the highest posts of government, the tribunals of justice, and the general administration of public affairs.

No one is allowed to marry out of his own caste, or to exchange one profession or trade for another, or to follow more than one business. An exception is made in favour of the philosopher, who for his virtue is allowed this privilege. "

Alberuni who wrote an account of his travels in India some time about 1030 AD must have been struck by the peculiarity of the Hindu social organisation. For he too has not omitted to make a note of it in the record of impressions he made. He observed: --

"The Hindus call their castes varna i.e. colours, and from a genealogical point of view they call them jataka i.e., births. These castes are from the very beginning only four.

1. The highest caste is the Brahmins of whom the books of the Hindus tell that they were created from the head of Brahma. And a Brahma is only another name for the force called nature, and the head is the highest part of the animal body, the Brahmans are the choice part of the whole genus. Therefore the Hindus consider them as the very best of mankind.

II. The next caste is the Kshatriyas, who were created, as they say, from the shoulders and hands of Brahma. Their degree is not much below that of the Brahman.

III. After them follow the Vaishyas, who were created from the thigh of Brahma.

IV. The Sudras, who were created from his feet. Between the latter two classes there is no very great distance. Much, however, as these classes differ from each other, they live together in the same towns and villages, mixed together in the same houses and lodgings.

After the Shudras follow the people called Antyaja, who render various kinds of services, who are not reckoned amongst any caste, but only as members of a certain craft or profession. There are eight classes of them who freely intermarry with each other, except the fuller, shoemaker and weaver, for no others would condescend to have anything to do with them. These eight guilds are the fuller, shoemaker, juggler, the basket and shield maker, the sailor, fisherman, the hunter of wild animals and of birds, and the weaver. The four castes do not live together with them in one and the same place. These guilds live near the villages and towns of the four castes, but outside them.

The people called Hadi, Doma (Domba), Candala, and Badhatau (sic) are not reckoned amongst any caste or guild. They are occupied with dirty work, like the cleansing of the villages and other services. They are considered as one sole class, and distinguished only by their occupations. In fact, they are considered like illegitimate children; for according to general opinion they descend from a Sudra father and a Brahmani mother as the children of fornication; therefore they are degraded outcastes.

The Hindus give to every single man of the four castes characteristic names, according to their occupations and modes of life, eg., the Brahman is in general called by this name as long as he does his work staying at home. When he is busy with the service of one fire, he is called ishtin; if he serves three fires, he is called Agnihotrin; if he besides offers an offering to the fire, he is called Dikshita. And as it is with the Brahmana, so is it also with the other castes. Of the classes beneath the castes, the Hadi are the best spoken of, because they keep themselves free from everything unclean. Next follow the Doma, who play on the lute and sing. The still lower classes practise as a trade killing and the inflicting of judicial punishments. The worst of all are the Badhantan, who not only devour the flesh of dead animals, but even of dogs and other beasts.

Each of the four castes, when eating together, must form a group of themselves, one group not being allowed to comprise two men of different castes. If, further, in the group of the Brahman there are two men who live at enmity with each other, and the seat of the one is by the side of the other, they make a barrier between the two seats by placing a board between them, or by spreading a piece of dress, or in some other way; and if there is only a line drawn between them, they are considered as separated. Since it is forbidden to eat the remains of a meal, every single man must have his own food for himself, for if anyone of the party who are eating should take of the food from one and the same plate, that which remains in the plate becomes, after the first eater has taken part, to him who wants to take as the second, the remains of the meal as such is forbidden. "

Alberuni did not merely content himself with recording what struck him as peculiar in the Hindu social organization. He went on to say:—

" Among the Hindus institutions of this kind abound. We Muslims, of course, stand entirely on the other side of the question, considering all men as equal, except in piety; and this is the greatest obstacle which prevents any approach or understanding between Hindus and Muslims. "

Duarte Barbosa who was a Portuguese official in the service of the Portuguese Government in India from 1500 to 1571 has left a record of his impressions of Hindu society. This is what struck him in. Speaking of the kingdom of Gujerat:

" And before this kingdom Guzerate fell into the hands of the Moors. A certain caste of Heathen whom the Moors called Resbutos (Rajputs) dwelt therein, who in those days were the knights and wardens of the land, and made war wheresoever it was needful. These men kill and eat sheep and fish and all other kinds of food; in the mountains there are yet many of the them, where they have great villages and obey not the king of Guzarate, but rather wage daily war against him; who, do what he may, is yet not able to prevail against them, nor will do so, for they are very fine horsemen, and good archers, and have besides divers other weapons to defend themselves withal against the Moors, on whom they make war without ceasing; yet have they no king nor lord over them. And in this kingdom there is another sort of Heathen whom they call Baneanes, who are great merchants and traders. They dwell among the Moors with whom they carry on all their trade. This people eat neither flesh nor fish nor anything subject to death; they slay nothing, nor are they willing even to see the slaughter of any animal; and thus they maintain their idolatry and hold it so firmly that it is a terrible thing. For often it is so that the Moors take to them live insects or small birds, and make as though to kill them in their presence, and the Baneanes buy these and ransom them, paying much more than they are worth, so that they may save their lives and let them go. And if the King or a Governor of the land has any man condemned to death, for any crime which he has committed, they gather themselves together and buy him from justice, if they are willing to sell him, that he may not die. And divers Moorish mendicants as well, when they wish to obtain alms from this people, take great stones wherewith they beat upon their shoulders and bellies as though they would slay themselves before them, to hinder which they give them great alms that they may depart in peace. Others carry knives with which they slash their arms and legs, and to these too they give large alms that they may not kill themselves. Others go to their doors seeking to kill rats and snakes for them, and to them also they give much money that they may not do so. Thus they are much esteemed by the Moors. When these Baneanes meet with a swarm of ants on the road they shrink back and seek for some way to pass without crushing them. And in their houses they sup by daylight, for neither by night nor by day will they light a lamp, by reason of certain little flies which perish in the flame thereof; and if there is any great need of a light by night they have a lantern of varnished paper or cloth, so that no living thing may find its way in, and die in the flame. And if these men breed many lice they kill them not, but when they trouble them too much they send for certain men, also Heathen, who living among them and whom they hold to be men of a holy life, they are like hermits living with great abstinence through devotion to their gods. These men house them, and as many lice as they catch they place on their own heads and breed them on their own flesh, by which they say they do great service to their Idol. Thus one and all they maintain with great self restraint their law of not killing. On the other hand they are great usurers, falsifiers of weights and measures and many other goods and of coins ; and great liars. These Heathen are tawny men, tall and well-looking gaily attired, delicate and moderate in their food. Their diet is of milk, butter, sugar and rice, and many conserves of divers sorts. They make much use of dishes of fruit and vegetables and pot herbs in their food. Wheresoever they dwell they have orchards and fruit gardens and many water tanks wherein they bathe twice a day, both men and women; and they say when they have finished bathing that they are clear of as many sins as they have committed up to that hour. These Baneanes grow very long hair, as women do with us, and wear it twisted up on the head and made into a knot, and over it a turban, that they may keep it always held together; and in their hair they put flowers and other sweet scented things.

They use to anoint themselves with white sandalwood mixed with saffron and other scents. They are very amorous people. They are clad in long cotton and silken shirts and are shod with pointed shoes of richly wrought cordwain; some of them wear short coats of silk and brocade. They carry no arms except certain very small knives ornamented with gold and silver, and this for two reasons; first because they are men who make but little use of weapons; and secondly, because the Moors defend them. "

And there is here another class of Heathen whom they call Brahmenes, who are priests among them, and persons who manage and rule their houses of prayer and idol-worship, which are of great size and have great revenues; and many of them also are maintained by alms. In these houses are great numbers of wooden Idols, and others of stone and copper and in these houses or monasteries they celebrate great ceremonies in honour of these idols, entertaining them with great store of candles and oil lamps, and with bells after our fashion. These Brahmans and Heathen have in their creed many resemblance to the Holy Trinity, and hold in great honour the relation of the Triune Three, and always make their prayers to God, whom they confess and adore as the true God, Creator and maker of all things, who is three persons and one God, and they say that there are many other Gods who are rulers under him, in whom also they believe. These Brahmans and Heathen wheresoever they find our churches enter them and make prayers and adoration to our Images, always asking for Santa Maria, like men who have some knowledge and understanding of these matters and they honour the Church as is our manner, saying that between them and us there is little difference. These men never eat anything subject to death, nor do they slay anything. Bathing they hold to be a great ceremony and they say that by it they are saved. " Speaking of the Kingdom of Calicut, Barbosa says:—

" There is also in this same kingdom of Calicut a caste of people called Brahmenes who are priests among them (as are the clergy among us) of whom I have spoken in another place. "

" These all speak the same tongue, nor can any be a Brahmene except he be the son of a Brahmene. When they are seven years of age they put over their shoulder a strip of two fingers in breadth of untanned skin with the hair on it of a certain wild beast, which they call Cryvamergam, which resembles a wild ass. Then for seven years he must not eat betel for which time he continues to wear this strap. When he is fourteen years old they make him a Brahmene, and taking off their leather strip they invest him with the cord of three strands which he wears for the rest of his life as a token that he is a Brahmene. And this they do with great ceremonial and rejoicing, as we do here for a cleric when he sings his first mass. Thereafter he may eat betel, but no flesh or fish. They have great honour among the Indians, and as I have already said, they suffer deaths for no cause whatsoever, their own headman gives them a mild chastisement. They marry once only in our manner, and only the eldest son marries, he is treated like the head of an entailed estate. The other brothers remain single all their lives. These Brahmenes keep their wives well guarded, and greatly honoured, so that no other man may sleep with them; if any of them die, they do not marry again, but if a woman wrongs her husband she is slain by poison. The brothers who remain bachelors sleep with the Nayre women, they hold it to be a great honour, and as they are Bramenes no woman refuses herself to them, yet they may not sleep with any woman older than themselves. They dwell in their own houses and cities, and serve as clergy in the houses of worship, whither they go to pray at certain hours of the day, performing their rituals and idolatries. "

" Some of these Brahmenes serve the kings in every manner except in arms. No man may prepare any food for the King except a Brahmene or his own kin; they also serve as couriers to other countries with letters, money or merchandise, passing wherever they wish to go in safety and none does them any ill, even when the kings are at war. These Brahmenes are learned in their idolatry and possess many books thereof. The Kings hold them in high esteem."

" I have already spoken many times of the Naiyars and yet I have not hitherto told you what manner of men they are. you are to know that in this land of Malabar there is another caste of people called Nayars and among them are noble men who have no other duty than to serve in war, and they always carry their arms where ever they go, some swords and shields, others bows and arrows, and yet others spears. They all live with the King, and the other great Lords; nevertheless all receive stipends from the King or from the great Lords with whom they dwell. None may become a Nayar, save only he who is of Nayar lineage. They are very free from stain in their nobility. They will not touch anyone of low caste. Nor eat nor drink save in the house of a Nayar. These men are not married, their nephews (sister's sons) are their heirs. The Nayar women of good birth are very independent, and dispose of themselves as they please with Brahmenes and Nayars, but they do not sleep with men of caste lower than their own under pain of death. When they reach the age of twelve years their mothers hold a great ceremony.

When a mother perceives that her daughter has attained that age, she asks her kinsfolk and friends to make ready to honour her daughter, then she asks of the kindred and especially of one particular kinsman or great friend to marry her daughter; this he willingly promises and then he has a small jewel made, which would contain a half ducat of gold, long like a ribbon, with a hole through the middle which comes out on the other side, strung on a thread of white silk. The mother then on a fixed day is present with her daughter gaily decked with many rich jewels, making great rejoicing with music and singing, and a great assembly of people.

Then the kinsmen or friend comes bringing that jewel, and going through certain forms, throws it over the girl's neck. She wears it as a token all the rest of her life, and may then dispose of herself as she wills. The man departs without sleeping with her inasmuch as he is her kinsman; if he is not, he may sleep with her, but is not obliged to do so. Thenceforward the mother goes about searching and asking some young men to take her daughter's virginity; they must be Nayars and they regard it among themselves as a disgrace and a foul thing to take a woman's virginity. And when anyone has once slept with her, she is fit for association with men.

Then the mother again goes about enquiring among other young Nayars if they wish to support her daughter, and take her as a Mistress so that three or four Nayars agree with her to keep her, and sleep with her, each paying her so much a day; the more lovers she has the greater is her honour Each of one of them passes a day with her from midday on one day till midday on the next day and so they continue living quietly without any disturbance or quarrels among them. If any of them wishes to leave her, he leaves her, and takes another and she also if she is weary of a man, she tells him to go, and he does go, or makes terms with her.

Any children they may have stay with the mother who has to bring them up, for they hold them not to be the children of any man, even if they bear his likeness, and they do not consider them their children, nor are they heirs to their estates, for as I have already stated their heirs are their nephews, sons of their sisters, (which rule whosoever will consider inwardly in his mind will find that it was established with a greater and deeper meaning than the common folk think) for they say that the Kings of the Nayars instituted it in order that the Nayars should not be held back from their service by the burden and labour of rearing children. "

" In this kingdom of Malabar there is also another caste of people whom they call Biabares, Indian Merchants, natives of the land. They deal in goods of every kind both in the seaports and inland, where ever their trade is of most profit. They gather to themselves all the pepper and ginger from the Nayars and husbandmen and off times they buy the new crops beforehand in exchange for cotton clothes and other goods, which they keep at the seaports. Afterwards they sell them again and gain much money thereby. Their privileges are such that the king of the country in which they dwell cannot execute them by legal process. "

" There is in this land yet another caste of folk known as Cuiavern. They do not differ from the Nayars, yet by reason of a fault, which they committed, they remain separate from them. Their business is to make pottery and bricks for roofing the houses of the Kings and idols, which are roofed with bricks instead of tiles; only these, for as I have already said, other houses are thatched with branches. They have their own sort of idolatry, and their separate idols. "

" There is another Heathen caste which they call Mainatos, whose occupation is to wash clothes for the Kings, Brahmenes and Nayars. By this they live, and may not take up any other."

" There is another lower caste than these which they call Caletis, who are weavers who have no other way of earning save by weaving of cotton and silk clothes, but they are low caste folk and have but little money, so that they clothe the lower races. They are apart by themselves and have their own idolatry. "

" Besides the castes mentioned above, there are eleven others lower than they with whom the others do not associate, nor do they touch them under pain of death; and there are great distinctions between one and another of them, preserving them from mixture with one another. The purest of all these low, simple folk they call Tuias. Their work is mainly that of tending the palm-groves and gathering the fruit thereof, and carrying it away for wages on their backs, for there are no beasts of burden in the land. "

" There is another caste still lower than these whom they call Manen (Mancu in the printed text) who neither associate with others nor touch them, nor do the other touch them. They are washermen for the common people, and makers of sleeping mats from which occupations all but they are barred; their sons must perforce follow the same trade; they have their own separate idolatry. "

"There is another caste in this land still lower whom they call Canaquas. Their trade is making buckles and umbrellas. They learn letters for purposes of astronomy, they are great astrologers, and foretell with great truth things that are to come; there are some lords who maintain them for this cause."

"There is also another lower caste, also Heathens, called Ageres. They are masons, carpenters, smiths, metal workers and some are goldsmiths, all of whom are of a common descent, and a separate caste, and have their idols apart from other folk. They marry, and their sons inherit their property, and learn their fathers' trade. "

"There is another caste still lower in this country called Mogeres, they are almost the same as the Tuias, but they do not touch one another. They work as carriers of all things belonging to the Royal State when it moves from one place to another, but there are very few of them in this land; they are a separate caste; they have no marriage law; the most of them gain their living on the sea, they are sailors, and some of them fishers; they have no idols. They are as well slaves of the Nayars:

"There is another caste yet lower whom they call Monquer, fishers who have no other work than fishing, yet some sail in the Moors' ship and in those of other Heathens, and they are very expert seamen. This race is very rude, they are shameless thieves; they marry and their sons succeed them, their women are of loose character, they sleep with anyone whosoever and it is held no evil. They have their own idolatry. "

" In this land of Malabar there is another caste of Heathen even lower than those, whom, they call Betunes. Their business is salt-making and rice growing, they have no other livelihood."

" They dwell in houses standing by themselves in the fields away from the roads, whither the gentlefolk do not walk. They have their own idolatry. They are slaves of the Kings and Nayars and pass their lives in poverty. The Nayars make them walk far away from them and speak to them from a far off. They hold no intercourse with any other caste. "

" There is another caste of Heathen, even lower and ruder, whom they call Paneens, who are great sorcerers and live by no other means. "

"There is another caste lower and ruder than they, named Revoleens a very poor folk, who live by carrying firewood and grass to the towns, they may touch none, nor may any touch them under pain of death. They go naked, covering only their private parts with scant and filthy rags, the more part of them indeed with leaves of certain trees. Their women wear many brass rings in their ears; and on their necks, arms and legs, necklaces and bracelets of heads."

"And there is yet another caste of Heathens lower than these whom they call Poleas, who among all the rest are held to be accursed and excommunicate; they dwell in the fields and open campaigns in secret lurking places, whither folk of good caste never go save by mischance, and live in huts very strut and mean. They are tillers of rice with buffaloes and oxen. They never speak to the Nayars save from a far off, shouting so that they may hear them, and when they go along the roads they utter loud cries that they may be let past, and whosoever hears them leaves the road, and stands in the wood till they have passed by; and if anyone whether man or woman, touches them, his kinsfolk slay them forthwith, and in vengeance therefore they slay Poleas until they are weary without suffering any punishment. "

" Yet another caste there is even lower and baser called Parens, who dwell in the most desert places away from all other castes. They have no intercourse with any person nor anyone with them; they are held to be worse than devils, and to be damned. Even to see them is to be unclean and outcaste. They eat yams and other roots of wild plants. They cover their middles with leaves, they also eat the flesh of wild beasts. "

"With these end the distinctions between the castes of the Heathen, which are eighteen in all, each one separate and unable to touch others or marry with them; and besides these eighteen castes of the Heathen who are natives of Malabar, which I have now related to you, there are others of outlandish folk merchants and traders in the land, where they possess houses and estates, living like the natives yet with customs of their own. "

These foreigners were not able to give a full and detailed picture of caste. This is understandable. For to every foreigner the private life of the Hindu is veiled and it is not possible for him to penetrate it. The social organism of India, the play of its motive forces, is moreover, regulated infinitely more by custom, carrying according to locality and baffling in its complexity, than by any legal formula which can be picked out of a legal text book. But there is no doubt that caste did appear to the foreigner as the most singular and therefore the most distinguishing feature of Hindu society. Otherwise they would not have noted its existence in the record they made of what they observed when they came to India.

Caste therefore is something special in the Hindu social organization and marks off the Hindus from other peoples. Caste has been a growing institution. It has never been the same at all times. The shape and form of Caste as it existed when Megashthenes wrote his account was very different from what the shape and form it had taken when Alberuni came and the appearance it gave to the Portuguese was different from what it was in the time of Alberuni. But to understand caste one must have more exact idea of its nature than these foreigners are able to give.

To follow the discussion of the subject of caste it is necessary to familiarise the reader with some basic conceptions which underlie the Hindu Social Organisation. The basic conception of social organisation which prevails among the Hindus starts with the rise of four classes or Varnas into which Hindu society is believed to have become divided. These four classes were named (1) Brahmins, the priestly and the educated class (2) Kshatriyas the military class (3) The Vaishyas the trading class and (4) The Shudras the servant class. For a time these were merely classes. After a time what were only classes (Varnas) became Castes (Jatis) and the four castes became four thousand. In this way the modern caste system was only the evolution of the ancient Varna system.

No doubt the caste system is an evolution of the Varna system. But one can get no diea of the caste system by a study of the Varna system. Caste must be studied apart from Varna.

II

An old agnostic is said to have summed up his philosophy in the following words:—

" The only thing I know is that I know nothing; and I am not quite sure that I know that "

Sir Denzil lbbetson undertaking to write about caste in the Punjab said that the words of this agnostic about his philosophy expressed very exactly his own feelings regarding caste. It is no doubt true that owing to local circumstances there does appear a certain diversity about caste matters and that it is very difficult to make any statement regarding any one of the castes. Absolutely true as it may be, as regards one locality which will not be contradicted with equal truth as regards the same caste in some other area.

Although this may be true yet it cannot be difficult to separate the essential and fundamental features of caste from its non-essential and superficial features. An easy way to ascertain this is to ask what are the matters for which a person is liable to be excluded from caste. Mr. Bhattacharya has stated the following as causes for expulsion from caste. (1) Embracing Christanity or Islam (2) Going to Europe or America (3) Marrying a widow (4) Publicly throwing the sacred thread (5) Publicly eating beef, pork or fowl (6) Publicly eating kachcha food prepared by a Mahomedan, Christian or low caste Hindu (7) Officiating at the house of a very low caste Shudra (8) By a female going away from home for immoral purposes (9) By a widow becoming pregnant. This list is not exhaustive and omits the three most important causes which entail expulsion from caste.

They are (10) Intermarrying outside caste (II) Inter dining with persons of another caste and (12) Change of occupation. The second defect in the statement of Mr. Bhattacharya is that it does not make any distinction between essentials and non-essentials. Of course, 'when a person is expelled from his caste the penalty is uniform. His friends, relatives and fellowmen refuse to partake of his hospitality. He is not invited to entertainment in their houses. He cannot obtain brides or bridegrooms for his children. Even his married daughters cannot visit him without running the risk of being excluded from caste. His priest, his barber and washermen refuse to serve him. His fellow caste men severe their connection with him so completely that they refuse to assist him even at the funeral of a member of his household. In some cases the man excluded from caste is debarred access to public temples and to the cremation or burial ground.

These reasons for expulsion from caste indirectly show the rules and regulations of the caste. But all regulations are not fundamental. There are many which are unessential. Caste can exist even without them. The essential and unessential can be distinguished by asking another question. When can a Hindu who has lost caste regain his caste ? The Hindus have a system of Prayaschitas which are Penances and which a man who has been expelled from caste must perform before he can be admitted to caste fellowship. With regard to these Prayaschitas or Penances certain points must be remembered. In this first place, there are caste offences for which there is no Prayaschita. In the second place, the Prayaschitas vary according to the offence. In some cases the Prayaschitas involve a very small penalty. In other cases the penalty involved is a very severe one.

The existence of a Prayaschita and the absence of it have a significance which must be clearly understood. The absence of Prayaschita does not mean that anyone may commit the offence with impunity. On the contrary it means that the offence is of an immeasurable magnitude and the offender once expelled is beyond reclamation. There is no re-entry for him in the caste from which he is expelled. The existence of a Prayaschita means that the offence is compoundable. The offender can take the prescribed prayaschita and obtain admission in the caste from which he is expelled.

There are two offences for which there is no penance. These are (1) change from Hindu Religion to another religion (2) Marriage with a person of another caste or another religion. It is obvious if a man loses caste for these offences he loses it permanently.

Of the other offences the prayaschitas prescribed are of the severest kind, are two—(1) interdining with a person of another caste or a non-Hindu and (2) Taking to occupation which is not the occupation of the caste. In the case of the other offences the penalty is a light one almost nominal.

The surest clue to find out what are the fundamental rules of caste and what caste consists it is furnished by the rules regarding prayaschitas. Those for the infringement of which there is no prayaschita constitute the very soul of caste and those for the infringement of which the prayaschita is of the severest kind make up the body of caste. It may therefore be said without any hesitation that there are four fundamental rules of caste. A caste may be defined as a social group having (a) belief in Hindu Religion and bound by certain regulations as to (b) marriage (c) food and (d) occupation. To this one more characteristic may be added namely a social group having a common name by which it is recognised.

In the matter of marriage the regulation lays down that the caste must be endogamous. There can be no intermarriage between members of different castes. This is the first and the most fundamental idea on which the whole fabric of the caste is built up.

In the matter of food the rule is that a person cannot take food from and dine with any person who does not belong to his caste. This means that only those who can intermarry can also inter dine. Those who cannot intermarry cannot inter dine. In other words, caste is an endogamous unit and also a communal unit.

In the matter of occupation the regulation is that a person must follow the occupation which is the traditional occupation of his caste and if the caste has no occupation then he should follow the occupation of his father.

In the matter of status of a person it is fixed and is hereditary. It is fixed because a person's status is determined by the status of the caste to which he belongs. It is hereditary because a Hindu is stamped with the caste to which his parents belonged, a Hindu cannot change his status because he cannot change his caste. A Hindu s born in a caste and he dies a member of the caste in which he is born. A Hindu may lose his status if he loses caste. But he cannot acquire a new or a better or different status.

What is the significance of a common name for a caste ? The significance of this will be clear if we ask two questions which are very relevant and a correct answer to each is necessary for a complete idea of this institution of caste. Social groups are either organised or unorganised. When the membership of the group and the process of joining and leaving the groups, are the subject of definite social regulations and involve certain duties and privileges in relation to other members of the group then the group is an organised group. A group is a voluntary group in which members enter with a full knowledge of what they are doing and the aims which the association is designed to fulfil. On the other hand, there are groups of which an individual person becomes a member without any act of volition, and becomes subject to social regulation and traditions over which he has no control of any kind.

Now it is hardly necessary to say that caste is a highly organised social grouping. It is not a loose or a floating body. Similarly, it is not necessary to say that caste is an involuntary grouping. A Hindu is born in a caste and he dies as a member of that caste. There is no Hindu without caste, cannot escape caste and being bounded by caste from birth to death he becomes subject to social regulations and traditions of the caste over which he has no control.

The significance of a separate name for a caste lies in this—namely it makes caste an organised and an involuntary grouping. A separate and a distinctive name for a caste makes caste asking to a corporation with a perpetual existence and a seal of separate entity. The significance of separate names for separate castes has not been sufficiently realised by writers on caste. In doing that they have lost sight of a most distinctive feature of caste. Social groups there are and they are bound to be in every society. Many social groups in many countries can be equated to various castes in India and may be regarded as their equivalent. Potters, Washermen, Intellectuals, as social groups are everywhere.

But in other countries they have remained as unorganised and voluntary groups while in India they have become organised and involuntary i.e., they have become castes because in other countries the social groups were not given name while in India they did. It is the name, which the caste bears which gives it fixate and continuity and individuality. It is the name which defines who are its members and in most cases a person born in a caste carries the name of the caste as a part of his surname. Again it is the name which makes it easy for the caste to enforce its rules and regulations. It makes it easy in two ways. In the first place, the name of the caste forming a surname of the individual prevents the offender in passing off as a person belonging to another caste and thus escape the jurisdiction of the caste. Secondly, it helps to identify the offending individual and the caste to whose jurisdiction he is subject so that he is easily handed up and punished for any breach of the caste rules.

This is what caste means. Now as to the caste system. This involves the study of the mutual relations between different castes. Looked at as a collection of caste, the caste system presents several features, which at once strike the observer. In the first place there is no inter-connection between the various castes, which form a system. Each caste is separate and distinct. It is independent and sovereign in the disposal of its internal affairs and the enforcement of caste regulations. The castes touch but they do not interpenetrate. The second feature relates to the order in which one caste stands in relation to the other castes in the system. That order is vertical and not horizontal.

Such is the caste and such is the caste system. Question is, is this enough to know the Hindu social organisation? For a static conception of the Hindu social organisation an idea of the caste and the caste system is enough. One need not trouble to remember more than the facts that the Hindus are divided into castes and that the castes form a system in which all hang on a thread which runs through the system in such a way that while encircling and separating one caste from another it holds them all as though it was a string of tennis balls hanging one above the other. But this will not be enough to understand caste as a dynamic phenomenon. To follow the workings of caste in action it is necessary to note one other feature of caste besides the caste system, namely class-caste system.

The relationship between the ideas of caste and class has been a matter of lively controversy. Some say that caste is analogous to class and that there is no difference between the two. Others hold that the idea of castes is fundamentally opposed to that of class. This is an aspect of the subject of caste about which more will be said hereafter. For the present it is necessary to emphasise one feature of the caste system which has not been referred to herein before. It is this. Although caste is different from and opposed to the notion of class yet the caste-system—as distinguished from caste—recognises a class system which is somewhat different from the graded status referred to above. Just as the Hindus are divided into so many castes, castes are divided into different classes of castes. The Hindu is caste-conscious. He is also class conscious. Whether he is caste conscious or class conscious depends upon the caste with which he comes in conflict. If the caste with which he comes in conflict is a caste within the class to which he belongs he is caste conscious. If the caste is outside the class to which he belongs he is class conscious. Anyone who needs any evidence on this point may study the Non-Brahmin Movement in the Madras and the Bombay Presidency. Such a study will leave no doubt that to a Hindu caste periphery is as real as class periphery and caste consciousness is as real as class-consciousness.

Caste, it is said, is an evolution of the Varna system. I will show later on that this is nonsense. Caste is a perversion of Varna. At any rate it is an evolution in the opposite direction. But while caste has completely perverted the Varna system it has borrowed the class system from the Varna system. Indeed the Class-caste system follows closely the class cleavages of the Varna system.

Looking at the caste system from this point of view one comes across several lives of class cleavage which run through this pyramid of castes dividing the pyramid into blocks of castes. The first line of cleavage follows the line of division noticeable in the ancient Chaturvarna system. The old system of Chaturvarna made a distinction between the first three Varnas, the Brahmins, Kshatriyas, Vaishyas and the fourth Varna namely the Shudra. The three former were classes as the Regenerate classes. The Shudra was held as the unregenerate class. This distinction was based upon the fact that the former was entitled to wear the sacred thread and study the Vedas. The Shudra was entitled to neither and that is why he was regarded as the unregenerate class. This line of cleavage is still in existence and forms the basis of the present day class division separating the castes which have grown out of the vast class of Shudras from those which have grown out of the three classes of Brahmins, the kshatriyas and Vaishyas. This line of class cleavage is the one which is expressed by the terms High Castes and Low Castes and which are short forms for the High Class Castes and Low Class Castes.

Next after this line of cleavage there runs through the pyramid a second line of class cleavage. It runs just below the Low Class Castes. It acts above all the castes born out of the four Varnas i.e., the High Castes as well as the low castes above the remaining castes, which I will merely describe as the ' rest '. This line of class cleavage is again a real one and follows the well-defined distinction which was a fundamental principle of the Chaturvarna system. The Chaturvarna system as is pointed out made a distinction between the four Varnas putting the three Varnas above the fourth. But it also made an equally clear distinction between those within the Chaturvarna and those outside the Chaturvarna. It had a terminology to express this distinction. Those within the Chaturvarna—high or low, Brahmin or Shudra were called Savarna i.e., those with the stamp of the Varna. Those outside the Chaturvarna were called Avarna i.e., those without the stamp of Varna. All the castes which have evolved out of the four varnas are called Savama Hindus—which is rendered English by the term Caste Hindus—The ' rest ' are the Avarnas who in present parlance spoken of by- Europeans as Non-caste Hindus i.e., those who are outside the four original castes or varnas.

Much that is written about the caste system has reference mostly to the caste-system among the Savama Hindus. Very little is known about the Avarna Hindus. Who are these Avarna Hindus, what is their position in Hindu Society, how are they related to the Savarna Hindus are questions to which no attention has so far been paid. I am sure that without considering these questions no one can get a true picture of the social structure the Hindus have built. To leave out the Class cleavage between the Savarna Hindus and the Avarna Hindus is to relate Grimm's Fairy Tale which leaves out the witches, the goblins and the orges.